What If? #3

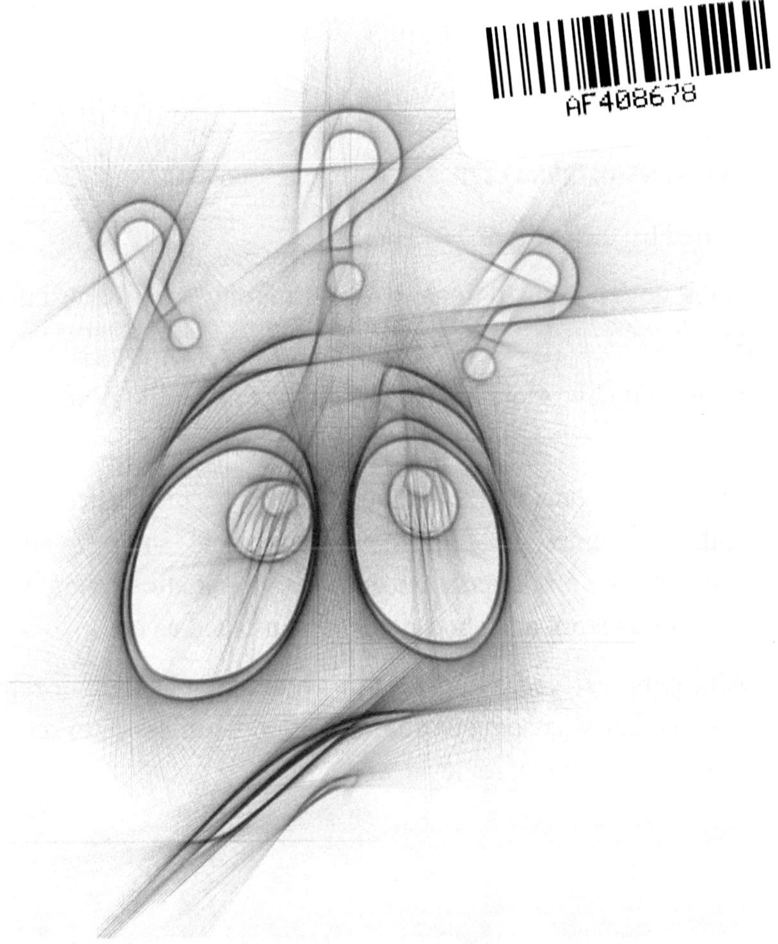

Dark fiction anthology by the GBBPub authors:

Erika M Szabo, Lorraine Carey, David W. Thompson, Martha Perez, Robert Allen Lupton, R.A. "Doc" Correa, and Shebat Legion

Stories

What if you think the known world isn't strange enough? Embark on a journey that pushes the boundaries, challenges your perception, and questions reason, logic, and established beliefs.

***

Midnight Murder by Erika M Szabo

Emma's trust in her psychic abilities solidified and she learned an important lesson about blind trust – even in those who she thought were closest to her.

Unexpected Trip by Lorraine Carey

A teacher faints at an Egyptian exhibit and has a vivid dream in Pompeii during the volcanic eruption. Was it a dream or did she travel through time?

Thy Sister's Blood by David W. Thompson

Friends on a haunted creek uncover ancient relations. Magic and mystery drive this journey of self-discovery with the enduring power of family.

The Ominous Sound of Stiletto Heels by Erika M Szabo

The sound of Madame Chloe's red stiletto heels in the hallways would quiet the students and teachers. When she walked by, an icy chill filled the air.

The Way to a Man's Heart by Shebat Legion

A Siren demonstrates her full vocal range, much to the dismay of a man caught in a trap of his own design.

Shadowman by Erika M Szabo

Their ultimate goal is a brighter future for all humanity. A world free of destruction and chaos.

Careful What You Wish For by David W. Thompson

At last, Victor finds his dream girl! But is it a match made in heaven or a far darker place? Love conquers all... or the dream becomes a nightmare.

Happily Ever After, and After by Shebat Legion

A woman revisits memories that are all too real, or are they? What makes a memory real?

I Love You Forever by Martha Perez

Can their love endure? Nicole, battling cancer, finds hope with Noah. Will they overcome life's challenges and keep their vow to love forever?

Jimmy's Clown by David W. Thompson

Brothers stick together, and childhood pranks are soon forgotten. But old grudges can fade slowly or swell with age like the nose of a clown.

Eye of the Jaguar by Robert Allen Lupton

An explorer falls onto an altar stone. He wakes to an ancient nightmare of Mayan jaguar worship. Can he save his humanity and return to modern times?

Unsung Heroes y Erika M Szabo

If people knew what the biker gang did and were not expecting any reward or recognition, these unsung heroes would be celebrated by many.

The Prodigal Daughter by R.A. "Doc" Correa

Cassandra Lynn Anderson, a haunted young woman, learns the terrifying truth of her origin.

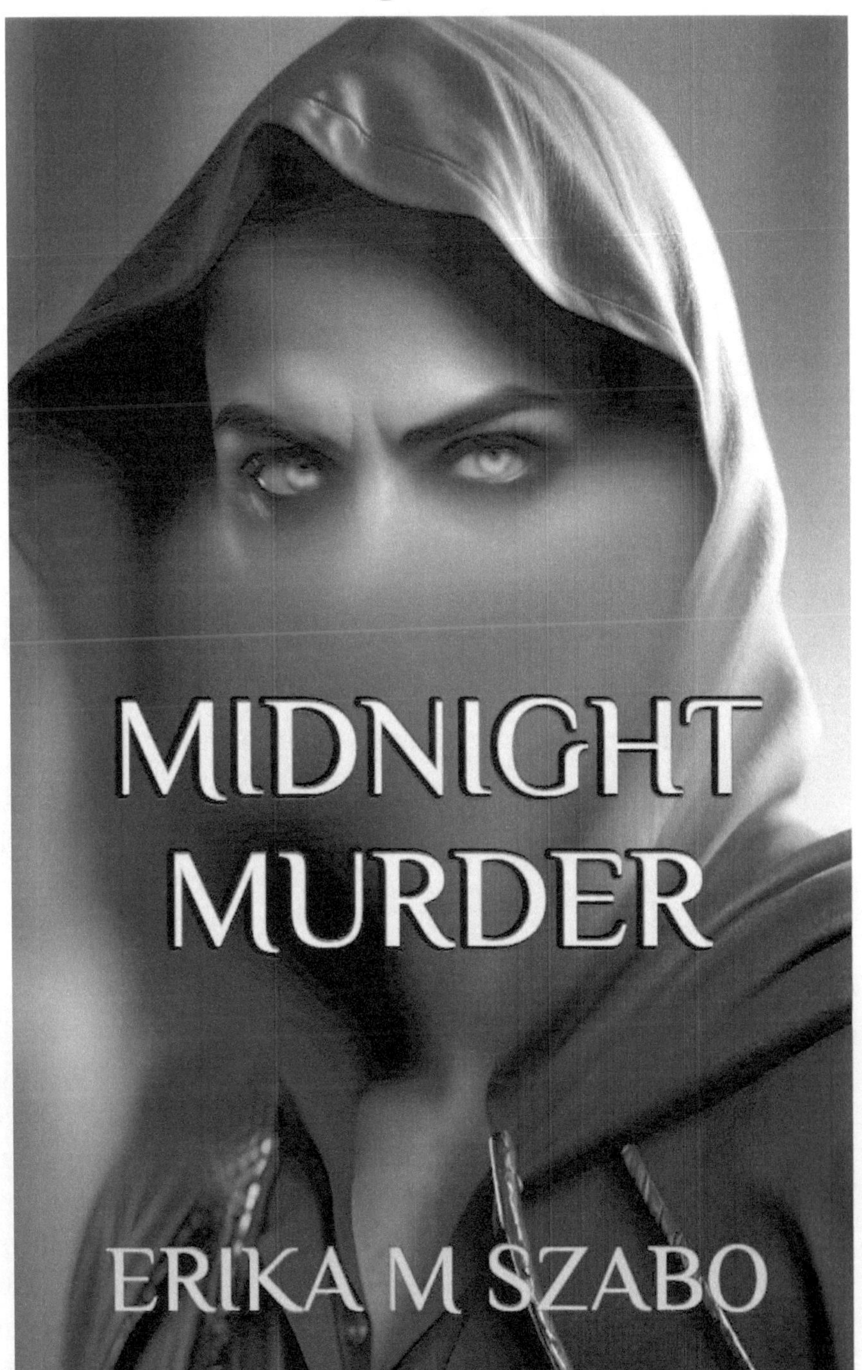
MIDNIGHT
MURDER
ERIKA M SZABO

Emma finished her patient notes and gave her report to the evening shift nurse before changing clothes and rushing to the garage. For once, she would be able to leave work on time. She thought back to days when she had to pull double shifts or when the chaos of the ER made it nearly impossible to finish her paperwork in a timely fashion. As she drove home, Emma called her husband.

"Are you working overtime again?" Paul asked with a laugh.

"No, for once I'll even have time to cook dinner," Emma replied.

"Wow, that's rare," Paul chuckled, knowing how often he had to work late at his law firm and rarely had time to finish his work before 5 pm. "Do you mind if I invite Steve over for dinner? He has an investment proposal and I'd rather discuss it at home than in the office."

"Of course, darling," Emma said with a bright, cheery tone. "Then I'll defrost the lasagna and take out the German cherry cake from the freezer that I picked up last week. It will give me time to tidy up before you arrive home."

"That sounds perfect, sweetheart! We'll be home by six."

On her way home, Emma couldn't resist stopping at a charming farmstand she passed by. She carefully selected fresh lettuce, crisp radishes, juicy tomatoes, and crunchy cucumbers to create a delicious salad.

As the food thawed, Emma tackled some light cleaning tasks around the house. She ran the vacuum over the carpets, dusted the surfaces, and even managed to squeeze in a quick shower before five o'clock rolled around. As she dried her hair, she tried to recall Steve's face. She had only met Paul's business manager once at a party nearly a year ago, and their exchange was brief and polite. Despite not knowing much about him, he seemed like a decent person and Paul had never said anything negative about him. The firm was successful and catered to affluent clients, a fact that Emma knew from casual conversations with her husband. Curiosity piqued as she wondered what kind of proposal Steve might have in store for them. Since their marriage three years ago, Emma made a conscious effort not to pry into Paul's work life and only knew snippets of information that he shared with her voluntarily.

Shortly after six, they arrived, but as soon as she looked at her husband's face, Emma knew something was wrong. The slight frown on his handsome features was a rare display of emotion for him, but Emma had learned to read his subtle signs over the years. His tense posture and the way he shot a quick glance at their guest, Steve, told her that something was very wrong. She raised her eyebrows in question but remained quiet and followed Paul's lead as they ushered Steve into the living room.

Paul expertly mixed cocktails for them all, but Emma could sense the tension in the air. As they sat down, Paul turned to Steve with a calm yet controlled demeanor. "Before you tell me about your investment plans, let me ask you something," he said in a low voice.

Emma watched with growing alarm as her husband's jaw tightened, signaling his underlying anger. She couldn't imagine what would come next. *It must be something very serious.* She thought. *Otherwise, he would talk about business after dinner, as he usually does.*

"Tell me about the two hundred thousand dollars," Paul's voice rose slightly, revealing his true emotions towards their guest.

Steve's hand shook and he jolted in his seat, spilling a few drops of his drink onto his lap. His eyes widened in surprise as Paul confronted him about missing money.

"Why are you asking me?" Steve stammered, trying to compose himself.

"Because the accountant called me just before we left to ask about one of our bank accounts," Paul explained. "He said he couldn't find the statement for the interest we had been paid on that account. I didn't want to cause a scene in the office, so I'm asking you now. Where is the money?"

"I had nothing to do with it!" Steve exclaimed, his face turning red with anger as he stood up. "Are you accusing me of something?"

"Yes!" Paul fumed, his frustration evident. "I checked with the bank, and they informed me that the account we had 210 thousand dollars in now only has eight thousand. What did you do with the missing money?"

"I… I'm leaving! You can't just accuse me of something I didn't do," Steve mumbled, putting his glass on the coffee table.

"You're not going anywhere until you answer my question!"

Paul's voice echoed through the room, loud and forceful as he jumped up to block Steve's path toward the door. Emma shrunk back into the far corner of the sofa, her heart racing as she watched them. Paul, usually calm and collected, now had a fiery rage burning in his eyes. She had never seen him like this before.

Steve looked like a cornered animal, his hands shaking, and his face twisted in fear. "Okay, I gamble, and I've been unlucky the past three months! I'm an addict. I'm sick!" he screamed; desperation evident in his voice. "I'll pay it back, just give me a chance."

Paul's voice cracked with pain as he spoke. "How could you do this? I trusted you!"

"I'm so sorry! You have to understand. It's a disease!" Steve pleaded, tears streaming down his face.

But Paul was unfazed. "You played your card, now you suffer the consequences. You're fired!" He stepped aside to let Steve pass. "And you'll have to pay back the money you stole," Paul said coldly.

Panic set in for Steve as he realized what that meant. Desperation swept over him as he begged, "You can't! Please, you can't do this to me."

Paul's face hardened, his once friendly features now twisted into a cold, angry mask. "You did this to yourself. Now get out of my house!"

Steve recoiled at the sharpness in Paul's voice, feeling a surge of pain and anger bubbling up inside him. He looked into Paul's eyes, but all he could see was disappointment and hurt. With drooping shoulders and a defeated expression, he turned and made his way to the door, the sound of his footsteps echoing in the tense silence between them.

"I trusted him," Paul whispered when the door closed behind Steve, his voice hoarse and heavy with emotion. He slumped down beside Emma, his shoulders shaking with the weight of betrayal.

Emma searched for the right words to console her husband, but they seemed to wither in her throat. Instead, she simply wrapped her arms around him, holding him close as they sat in a heavy silence.

The following days were grueling for both of them. Steve had disappeared without a trace, leaving them with unanswered questions and mounting debts.

Paul was forced to deplete the law firm's other accounts just to cover the unpaid bills, leaving them in a precarious financial situation. Tension hung thick in their home, and Emma could see the worry etched into every line on Paul's face.

"Where do you think he is?" Emma asked.

"Nobody knows. Maybe in another state, or in another country. If I were in his shoes, I would be ashamed to show my face too. It's not even about the money," Paul admitted one evening as they sat on the couch. "Money can be replaced. It's the disappointment that cuts deep - in him and in myself for missing the signs. I was so consumed with cases that I entrusted him to handle the firm's finances." His eyes held a mix of regret and frustration, and Emma squeezed his hand in understanding.

***

Emma grew accustomed to Paul arriving home late each night. She knew he was filling in for Steve's job until a replacement could be found, so she accepted his long hours with understanding. She had

9

become accustomed to eating dinner alone and going to bed alone in their silent apartment.

But one night, her peaceful slumber was abruptly interrupted by the shrill ring of her phone. Bleary-eyed and disoriented, she squinted at the caller ID and recognized it as Clarice's number. The two had been best friends since childhood and Clarice lived in the building next door. Still half-asleep, Emma fumbled and managed to hit the accept button with shaking fingers. "He's dead!" She was jolted awake by Clarice's frantic scream on the other end of the line.

"What? Who?" Emma croaked out, sitting up in bed and swinging her feet to the floor. "Where are you?"

"I... I'm on the street," Clarice stammered, panic evident in her voice. "I called the police. He's dead!"

Emma's heart raced as she struggled to make sense of Clarice's words. "Who is dead?" she asked in terror, as images of everyone she knew flashed through her mind. Quickly pulling on her slippers and yanking up her jeans, Emma braced herself for whatever awaited her on the other side of her apartment door.

"Hurry!" Clarice moaned and choked up, her sobs echoing through the phone. Emma's heart raced as she listened to her best friend's distraught voice. Without a second thought, she ran out of her second-floor apartment, slamming the door behind her in haste. Her chestnut hair flew wildly behind her as she took the steps two at a time, determined to reach Clarice as quickly as possible.

As she burst into the lobby and rushed towards the front door, Emma could hear Clarice's cries growing louder. "Stay with me, Clarice! I'm coming," she shouted into the phone, hoping her words would provide some comfort to her friend.

But as Emma swung open the front door and stepped outside, she froze in shock. Police cars screeched to a halt in front of the building, their flashing blue and red lights casting an eerie glow over the usually tranquil neighborhood.

The normally peaceful sidewalk was now filled with chaos. Her best friend, Clarice, knelt by a seemingly lifeless body, her hands covered in blood. Emma's eyes widened in disbelief as she noticed a long blade bloody knife resting on the ground by Clarice's knee.

Her mind raced as she tried to process what could have possibly led to this gruesome scene. She could feel her heart pounding in her chest as she looked at Clarice's tear-stained face and then down at the lifeless body. The realization hit her like a ton of bricks - *Clarice had killed Brian.*

"What...how did...what did you do?" Emma stuttered, unable to believe what she was seeing. As if in slow motion, Clarice turned to look at Emma with haunted eyes and whispered, "I didn't! I swear! How could you think I did?" Clarice looked up at her with deep betrayal and hurt flashing in her eyes.

"It's Paul!" Emma cried out when she recognized the man with a bloody wound in the middle of his chest and dropped to her knees. She hugged her husband's still body to her chest. "It's Paul! How did he get here?" Emma sobbed hysterically, knowing that her husband always used the elevator from the garage to go up to their apartment. "This is not happening!" she screamed.

"I… I don't know!" Clarice shrieked, shaking her head. "I was… I just found him like this."

As the officers cautiously approached, Clarice lifted her tear-stained face to meet their gaze. Her hands, stained with blood, trembled as she held them up in a pitiful attempt to show her innocence. After assessing the scene and asking a barrage of initial questions, the officers finally took Clarice away in handcuffs. Emma watched with a heavy heart, feeling like she was in a dream. The reality of the situation slowly sank in and she couldn't believe how drastically her life had changed in just a few moments. Everything she thought she knew had been shattered, leaving her feeling numb and lost.

***

The days blurred together for Emma, each one blending into the next as she sat alone in her bedroom. The once comforting walls now felt stifling and oppressive, as if they were closing in on her. She stared at them, hoping to make sense of it all.

Her best friend, whom she had known since they were children, was now behind bars, accused of murdering her husband. Emma couldn't wrap her head around it. It seemed impossible that someone so kind and gentle could commit such a heinous act.

But there were unanswered questions that plagued Emma's mind. Clarice kept insisting that she didn't kill him. Was she telling the truth? And if she did do it, what could have driven her to such a desperate and violent act?

Emma's parents tried their best to be supportive, but they too were struggling with their own emotions. They couldn't understand how their daughter's beloved friend could do something so horrific.

As the shock of Paul's funeral began to wear off, Emma grew restless. She needed answers. She went to the detective assigned to the case but got nowhere. So, with determination and a heavy heart, she mustered up the courage to visit Clarice in jail.

The visitation room was bleak and sterile, the cold air filled with tension and sadness. But Emma hardly noticed as she sat across from Clarice, who looked like a mere shell of the person she used to be. Their conversation was initially strained and awkward, but eventually, Clarice opened up and shared her side of the story with Emma.

Emma listened intently as her friend's tearful voice trembled while recounting the events that led up to the fateful night. Clarice's words were like shards of glass, piercing through Emma's heart with their painful honesty. "I never told you about how Brian treated me, I was too ashamed," she whispered, her voice barely audible above her sobs. "You and Paul were so happy together, and... I was foolishly hoping that Brian would change. But he didn't..." Clarice sighed, tears streaming down her face as she continued. "The months of verbal abuse and constant belittling finally pushed me over the edge. And then at a party, when you had a headache and went home alone, I confided in Paul."

Emma felt a surge of anger rising within her. "What happened?" she asked coldly, already imagining the worst.

"We just talked," Clarice confessed, her voice quivering with shame and regret. "But later... um, we started seeing each other more and more."

"What?" Emma's hand involuntarily slapped against the table in anger before she could stop it. She stood up abruptly, causing the guard standing nearby to take a step forward.

"I'm sorry! Everything is under control," Emma forced a smile through gritted teeth as she sat back down. But inside, she seethed with rage.

The guard's eyes narrowed suspiciously as he stood in front of the door. "One more outburst and she goes back to her cell," he warned, his hand resting on the doorknob.

"I'll be quiet. I promise!" Emma pleaded, her eyes wide with desperation as she turned to Clarice.

"Tell me everything!" she demanded, her voice quivering with a mix of fear and anger.

Clarice took a deep breath, her hands trembling at her sides as she glanced between Emma and the guard. "I know you're going to hate me, but I must tell you the truth."

Emma's jaw clenched as she waited for Clarice to continue.

"In this moment of hesitation, Clarice's voice shook as she revealed her deepest secret. "I was consumed by jealousy of your happiness, and I wanted just a taste of what you had. When Paul told me he was giving a lecture in New York a few weeks ago, I impulsively flew there and stayed at the same hotel as him. And then...we had dinner. As we talked about Brian and my tears flowed, Paul consoled me and one thing led to another..."

Emma leaned forward, her eyes blazing with fury. "One thing led to another?"

Clarice hung her head in shame. "I know it sounds terrible, but we both felt guilty afterward and it never happened again. Only that one time. I'm so sorry."

Emma's eyes narrowed into slits as she shot a murderous look at Clarice, but she fought to contain her boiling emotions. "Am I that stupid?" she hissed, "I didn't notice anything, and Paul didn't say a word about this...this affair!"

Clarice's lower lip quivered as she confessed, "I meant to tell you, but I was afraid and felt guilty. I knew if I said anything, you'd kick Paul out. I didn't want to ruin your happy life."

"But Paul," Emma sniffed, her voice cracking with emotion. "How could he do this to me? How could he act like nothing happened? He lied to me!"

"Don't blame him," Clarice whispered, tears welling up in her eyes. "I begged him not to tell you."

"And he complied," Emma bitterly admitted, "keeping up with his lies so masterfully. I'm more disappointed in his actions than yours." She let out a shaky breath before commanding, "Tell me what happened the night he died." The words felt like knives on her tongue, but she needed to know the truth.

"Brian and I had a huge fight," Clarice recalled with a shaky voice. "It was brutal. He broke into my phone and read Paul's text messages. The anger in his eyes was like fire, burning me from the inside out. He called me all kinds of names, hit me, and stormed out yelling that he'll make me pay for that. My heart pounded as I tried to process what had just happened. In a panic, I called Paul, my thoughts racing as I heard his voice on the other end.

He told me to meet him in the lobby of our building, but when I arrived, he wasn't there. Fear gripped me as I stepped outside and walked toward your building. And that's when I saw him - Paul lying on the sidewalk, motionless and pale. I was so scared, but I dialed 911 and started performing CPR. "I didn't kill him, Emma! I swear! I... I loved him."

"And then you called me."

"I didn't know what else to do. But now the detectives are convinced that I'm the killer because my fingerprints are on the knife. But I don't understand why... why did I pick up the knife? It was covered in blood next to Paul's body when I found him. You believe me, don't you?"

Emma sighed heavily and stood up, torn between her loyalty to her friend and the evidence against her. "I want to believe you, Clarice. But right now, it's hard for me to."

"I think Brian killed him to frame me. Don't you think?"

"I don't know. Maybe…"

"I told the detectives, but they just dismissed me because my fingerprints are on the knife." Clarice cried out in despair.

***

Emma leaned back in her worn armchair; her gaze fixed on the raindrops streaking down the windowpane. The room was shrouded in silence, save for the occasional muffled tap of rain against the glass. Emma felt a familiar tingle at the base of her neck - a signal from her psychic intuition that something significant was trying to come out.

A wave of unease washed over Emma's body, settling deep in her stomach and refusing to be ignored. She knew she needed to delve deeper into the cryptic messages swirling in her mind, but it was as if an invisible force held her back. And then, in a moment of eerie clarity, a vivid image consumed her thoughts.

She saw a sinister silhouette lurking in the shadows of an ancient oak tree, fixated on a man standing on the sidewalk. The standing man was Paul. The man behind the tree fidgeted nervously; his eyes locked on the entrance of a nearby building as if he were waiting for someone. But before Emma could make sense of it all, she watched in horror as the curtain in a first-floor window was pulled aside and the figure hiding behind the tree suddenly launched itself at Paul.

As their eyes met, Emma could feel a coldness wash over her - a malevolence emanating from this unknown assailant. His face was blurred, yet she could see the sinister glint in his eyes as he charged towards Paul with deadly intent.

After a few minutes, her vision cleared and she took deep breaths, feeling the tension ease from her body. With fierce determination etched on her face, she focused all of her energy on the enigmatic puzzle presented by her visions. *Someone had seen the murder from the first-floor window.*

Her hands trembled with excitement as she fumbled for a pen and paper, desperate to capture every fleeting detail etched in her mind. This meager fragment could be the key to unraveling the haunting mystery.

The soft glow of her laptop provided the only source of light in the dimly lit room. She meticulously combed through countless news reports, connecting dots and piecing together clues from the psychic messages that had flooded her mind. But no matter how hard she tried, she couldn't find any connections.

Sitting at her cluttered desk, she was surrounded by a wall plastered with a mosaic of newspaper clippings and meticulous notes. Emma wished she could see the man's face in her vision. She wondered if it was Brian or a random stranger. *No, it wasn't a random robbery gone wrong. Paul's valet was in his pocket with his iPhone, and his expensive watch was still on his arm when he was killed.*

***

Despite her parents' desperate pleas to abandon the search and return to a normal routine, Emma felt an unshakable sense of duty weighing heavily on her shoulders. The visions that plagued her every waking moment seemed to demand action, warning her that ignoring them would only prolong their haunting presence. With a fierce determination burning in her chest, Emma defied all advice and boldly approached the detective with the scant evidence she had collected about the possible eyewitness.

The detective's initial expressions were guarded and cautious as Emma recounted her visions in vivid detail. His eyes flickered with skepticism, but as she continued to describe the scene and events with unwavering confidence, his features slowly transformed from doubt to intrigue. She could see the spark of curiosity ignite in his gaze as he leaned forward, fully engrossed in her tale.

Fueled by determination, the detective relentlessly searched for any physical evidence or witnesses to corroborate Emma's claims. With a dogged focus, they probed for more information, leaving no stone unturned. But all Emma had were fragments of her vision, haunting images that refused to solidify into proof or lead to any substantial leads.

Still, something about Emma's conviction and intensity compelled the detective to take her seriously. With newfound determination, they decided to follow up on her lead and see where it would take them.

Emma desperately strained her mind, trying to recall every minute detail of her vision. But the killer's face remained an enigma, a hazy figure lurking in the shadows of her thoughts. The more she tried to grasp onto it, the deeper it seemed to slip away. A chilling sensation settled in her gut as she realized she was missing a crucial piece of the puzzle - one that could mean life or death for Clarice.

***

As the darkness of sleep enveloped her, Emma's mind was once again transported to a vivid, mysterious world. This time, the images were clearer and more defined than ever before. She saw a man with

17

wild eyes and frantic movements running through the dense trees and bushes in the park behind their building on the night of Paul's murder. The sound of his heavy breathing echoed in her ears as he frantically searched for an escape route.

Far from the beaten path, in her vision, Emma followed the man's frantic footsteps until they led her to a small cabin hidden deep within the dark and foreboding woods. Her heart pounding in her chest, she cautiously approached the dilapidated structure, sensing that this was where the answers lay.

As she peered through a broken window, her blood ran cold at what she saw – the murderer's face staring back at her with chilling malice. A wave of terror washed over Emma as she realized that this was no ordinary dream; it was a message sent by her psychic abilities – one that could potentially solve Paul's murder.

With renewed determination, Emma went to the police station early morning and recounted every detail of what she had seen in her psychic dream. The detective's eyes narrowed in concentration as he asked questions, trying to piece together the puzzle. However, when they brought in the woman from the apartment that Emma had seen in her vision, she adamantly denied seeing anything out of the ordinary. Disappointment weighed heavily on the detective's face. But Emma was determined not to let this lead go cold.

She visited the woman at her home and pleaded with her to tell the truth to the detective. After some hesitation, the woman finally broke down and admitted to seeing the murder take place from her window. She had been too scared to say anything before, knowing that the killer was still out there somewhere. As she described the man who had taken Paul's life, Emma couldn't believe what she was hearing. It matched exactly with what she had seen in her vision.

Immediately, the detective organized a search of the nearby woods where Emma had seen the cabin in her vision. Sure enough, they came across a small cabin that fit her description perfectly. The team of officers moved silently; their breaths held as they crept up to the structure. One officer carefully peeked through the window and then quickly pulled back, signaling to the team leader that someone was inside.

"I saw a man sleeping on a cot," he mouthed to the leader, who wasted no time and instructed the team with hand signals to maneuver close to the small, rundown building, and stepping to the door, he kicked it.

The decaying wood splintered, succumbing to the weight of the officers as they swarmed into the small cabin. A disheveled man leaped off the cot, his eyes wide with fear and confusion.

"Steve Baldwin, you are under arrest for the brutal murder of Paul Hoggins," announced the leader of the group, his voice stern and unwavering. He proceeded to recite the Miranda rights as the other officers searched the room.

***

With a closer examination, they discovered that Steve's thumbprint matched the one found on the knife under the dried blood hidden by Clarice's fingerprints. It was clear evidence that Clarice had handled the murder weapon after the crime.

News of Steve's arrest spread like wildfire through their small town, bringing a sense of closure to both Emma and Clarice's families. Though it could never bring back Emma's beloved husband or repair her fractured friendship with Clarice, there was some solace in knowing that justice had been served.

For Emma, this experience solidified her belief in her psychic abilities and taught her an important lesson about blind trust – even in those who she thought were closest to her.

LORRAINE CAREY
UNEXPECTED
TRIP

Pompeii

"Valeria . . . Valeria, can you hear me?" a strange voice echoed as the young woman struggled to open her eyes seeing two tall young girls possibly in their late teens dressed in white togas at her side. "She's coming to," said one of the girls.

"Where . . . where am I?"

"You are in the House of the Vestals, my dear. You passed out a short time ago as you were working out in the garden on your jug and hit your head on one of the pedestals. You know you were told to avoid being in the sun too long with your fair skin," the first girl spoke.

"And who are you?"

Both girls looked at each other quizzically.

"I am Dalanya and this is Catania, your Vestal Sisters." Dalanya took her hand and helped Valeria to sit up on the cot.

"I don't remember any of this I tell you, the young woman claimed as she glanced around at her surroundings. Her eyes scanned the area that revealed tall pillars and large marble statues that led out to a massive courtyard with a huge fountain. "This has to be a dream! I mean—"

"Catania has sent for the Medicus. He should be here shortly," Dalanya said as she laid her hand on the woman's shoulder. "He'll know what to do."

An older man dressed in multicolored robes carrying a large satchel approached from the outside patio entering the small chamber. He had instructed Dalanya and Catania to inform him as to what had occurred.

"I know this young lady. She has simply fainted. I have treated her before for a similar condition. A vial of Posca is all she needs. She gets dehydrated easily. He pulled a small vial from his satchel and instructed her to drink, which she did.

She wiped her lips after chugging down the entire contents of the vial and gave the Medicus a skeptical look. "Exactly what's in that?" She scrunched up her nose showing her distaste for the drink.

"It's a mixture of vinegar, water, and herbs," he said.

"My name is Ramethius, the Medicus and I believe you may also have a slight concussion from hitting your head."

"Oh," the woman uttered as he checked her eyes and head using a strange instrument from his bag that managed to clamp open her eyes.

"Her pupils are not dilated but she still may have a slight concussion," he announced as he turned to the girls. "Best to keep an eye on her the rest of the day. Make sure you don't let her sleep."

"Why can't she remember who she is? Dalanya asked.

"Well, she's one of the oldest Vestals here, I mean—" Catania added. "Could be her age."

"It may be a temporary case of amnesia. It should return in time," Ramethius said as he secured his bag. "Now I must go as I'm needed at the House of Faun."

Both Dalanya and Catania sat next to Valeria giving her words of comfort but most of all encouraging her to rest.

"Your artwork can wait, Sister," Dalanya said, taking her hand. "You heard what the Medicus said."

"Rest . . . rest! I can't rest!" She shot up. "I have to finish my piece for the art show for Aulius Restituto. It will be featured among some of the other fine pieces here in Pompeii then grace the main hall of the house of Vetti."

The girls both looked at each other astounded. "Well then, I guess her amnesia has instantly returned," Dalanya said.

"It was probably the mention of artwork that brought her back," Catania said. "We both know how obsessive she is about that show she keeps talking about."

Valeria tried to rise from her cot but both girls gently pushed her back to a lying position. "You will rest here for a few hours."

Valeria reasoned she had to agree to the girls' wishes but knew once they were out of sight, she'd plan to get back to painting her jug.

She watched the girls walk through the archway that led out to the lush gardens. *I can only hope to see my beloved Marcus. I know he will be working in the kitchens today at the Vetti House. I long to feel his strong arms around me again. We've managed to keep this secret for some time now. Should we be caught- I'd be banned from the House of Vestals and he being a slave would be sentenced to death!*

Valeria felt a slight dizziness sensation overtake her and decided to sit for a while until it had passed. *I've got to finish that jug. Tomorrow is the show and I'll crawl if I have to get it over there.* She fiddled with her long black braid that hung to one side over her shoulder making sure the gold threads were securely in place that were weaved into the braid. A Vestal always had to look her best whenever she was out in the public eye.

"We both know what she's up to," Dalanya said as she and Catania walked through the garden.

"You mean that slave, Marcus that works over at the Vetti House?"

"Yes, Rumor has it she's been sneaking off to see him."

"It's true, and if she's caught, we both know the consequences both of them will face," Dalanya said as she bent down to smell the flowery scent of a hearty lilac bush.

"You going to tell on her?" Catania asked."

"No. I don't think we need to be known as spies here. Besides she is close to being released from her service very soon. She can be with Marcus all she wants then."

The ground shook with tremors and some of the larger garden pots had moved.

"Not that again!" Catania shouted. "This is the second time this week it's happened."

"Not to worry, it's very common as you well know, Dalanya said trying to calm her friend. That volcano has to release the pressure now and then, my friend. Now let's head over to the Temple of Isis and make sure all is well over there."

Valeria also felt the tremors as she tried to gain some steadiness to stand. "Great! Just what I need now," she murmured.

She slowly walked out to the garden checking to make sure the coast was clear to finish painting her jug. She breathed a sigh of relief when she saw that it was still there sitting atop a pedestal and her paint kit was left untouched. She needed to paint two more strands of ivy in a deep purple around the rim then decided on a few vertical lines that would run from the top to the bottom. But she knew she had to get some water as she would most likely be outside for another hour or so. She walked over to the aqueduct and filled up one of the many flasks that sat along the ledge by the wall.

Walking back to the garden she thought about her duties. It was her night to tend to the flame as well. It was the same duty that her Sisters in Rome had. Each Vestal took her turn. They all knew if that flame were to die out Rome would fall into disaster. It was their main mission. She planned on finishing her project before noon and taking it to the Vetti house.

Valeria stood back and admired her handiwork. The jug was stunning and the colors she'd used were vibrant. *This will surely be chosen to grace the main hall of the Vetti House*, she thought.

After making sure she looked suitable and was feeling better she grabbed her jug and headed off to the southernmost part of the city which was area V1 near the gate. She carried the jug by the handle and used her left hand to wipe the sweat off her forehead. The heat seemed to be intense but it was just a bit past noon. She passed several merchants on her way there who were making deliveries to the vast estate and others with various artwork as well.

Marcus should be in the kitchen area sweeping at this time, she thought as she quickened her step and her heart rate sped up. I want to show him this piece first. I've always valued his opinion on my art.

***

The Eruption

Two broad-shouldered Centurion guards nodded to Valeria signaling her to enter the courtyard freely. She glanced around watching a few other guests tour the grounds. They were well-dressed patricians donning red and golden togas and accompanied by Master Restituto.

Valeria's heart beat faster as she noticed the dark-haired portly man heading her way. "I'm assuming this piece is for the art event?"

"Yes, it is," she said humbly with a slight bow.

"Would you mind taking this over to the atrium at the far end?" he asked as he pointed the way.

Valeria walked toward the atrium but stopped halfway to turn around to see if Master Restituto was still occupied with his guests. She quickened her step still holding onto her prized piece. *Good, now I have time to stop over in the kitchen area and show him this jug.*

Upon entering the kitchen, she found Marcus sweeping with his back to her and another slave preparing a large tray of figs and other fruits. With his toga sagging far beyond his waist, Marcus's muscular build was an artwork in itself. She walked in and greeted both men. Marcus dropped his broom and walked over to her noting the other man was getting ready to leave the kitchen with the tray. "My dear Valeria. What are you doing here?"

"I . . . I wanted you to see my latest piece for the art event tomorrow. What do you think?" She held out the jug at arm's length, rotating the piece to display her intricate ivy designs.

25

"I think you are the most beautiful woman I've ever laid eyes on," he said running his hand along her silky long braid.

"You need to watch what you say, Marcus! You never know who's listening."

"There's no one around so no need to worry. Set this jug down here on the table so I can admire it along with your beauty."

"No need to worry? You say that so casually. You *do* know what would happen to both of us if we were caught; I'd lose my title as a Vestal and you would most likely be put to death!"

Marcus shook his head trying to dismiss the words she'd just spoken.

No sooner than she set the jug down the floor beneath them rumbled. Valeria reached to steady her jug for fear it would fall. "This is the second one we've had this week," she said.

"I know. I've heard the Masters speaking of how active the volcano has been lately. They have even spoken of leaving until it's safe to return."

"And where will you go?"

"I must stay here," he said smoothing his jet-black hair out of his eyes." It's my duty."

"Well, let's hope it calms down soon. I'm looking forward to this art show and seeing you again."

"Yes, I am as well." He moved in closer to kiss her as she parted her full lips.

"I must go now. I have to get this piece over to the atrium."

"Let me take it there for you," Marcus offered.

"How kind of you. And I guess I will see you tomorrow at the event." She placed her hand on his bare chest, the part that his sheath did not cover, feeling his toned muscles. "You should have been a god with that body."

Another stronger rumble came from beneath their feet causing Valeria to fall to the ground. Marcus helped her up. "We need to see what is happening, my love."

They walked out to the courtyard to see others scrambling about. Most were pointing to Mount Vesuvius as it was spewing ash and smoke in the distance.

Marcus took Valeria's hand, "You need to run. Go back to the temple house and see if your Sisters are boarding the boats to leave."

"I'm not leaving without you!"

"I will be okay. Trust me. Now go!" he yelled.

Valeria began to run out of the villa and onto the street toward the Vestal house when her sandal got caught in one of the cobblestones causing her to fall.

A stranger had helped her up telling her she needed to get to the harbor.

The strong smell of sulfur filled the air and people were coughing and covering their heads. She turned again to look back and black ash was pouring faster down toward the city. *This can't be happening! Maybe the gods are punishing me for breaking my vow,* she thought.

Now that she regained her stance, she continued her way toward the Vestal home. It was hard to move with so many people crowding the streets. Many were coughing with hands over their mouths, yet the screams could still be heard by many.

She turned the corner where the flower vendor had been and saw a young girl crouched down under a large tarp that shaded the small venue. She appeared to be around twelve years old. She was weeping. Valeria crouched down to assist the girl who had hidden her face amongst thick red locks. "Where are your parents, my dear?" Valeria asked, sweeping her hair out of her eyes.

The girl looked up, her green eyes swollen. "I . . . I went to our villa but no one was there. I ran out following the crowds but I got a pain in my side. I can't go on any further."

Valeria took her hand and pulled her up. "You can come with me. I am on my way to the Vestal home and then we will go with the others to the boats."

The young girl wiped her eyes with her delicate pale hand and rose to accompany Valeria.

The smoke was getting thicker, and it was hard to breathe or talk for that matter.

"What is your name, child?"

"It's Serena."

A tall older woman approached them from behind yelling Serina's name. "We've been looking for you!"

She grabbed the young girl's hand. "We must run now my daughter. There is no time left."

Valeria was relieved to see that the girl had found her mother. She watched them as they walked swiftly ahead only to see Serina turn around and mouth a 'thank you'.

Once she passed the baker's house, she knew she was almost home, but she turned around and knew in her heart what she had to do. *I can't and won't leave without Marcus.* She felt it hard to breathe and the heat had caused her to become weak. She found a small enclave to rest in. *I pray to the gods Marcus is still at the villa.*

Still feeling weak she managed to make it to the Vetti house but few were still there. Many had grabbed a few of their belongings in sacks and were headed out. She walked through the main hall and out to the gardens where she found Marcus attempting to cover one of the many statues.

"Marcus! We must leave now. Forget about this place."

He turned to her, "I thought you were headed to the Vestal house."

"No. I want to be with you," she said, her arms around his broad shoulders.

"Then we must leave now. Time is running out," he said.

Marcus and Valeria headed out on the street heading to the harbor but the smoke and ash had become intolerable. Valeria was having a hard time breathing and had to stop. Marcus had a bit more strength and sat with her against the wall leading to the boats. Marcus pulled Valeria up having her lean on his shoulder trying to get her to take a few more steps only to have her collapse there on the street.

Marcus knelt beside her knowing she wasn't going to make it. He himself was feeling the effects of the smoke now filling his lungs. Even in his weak state, he was able to speak. "I know we won't make it out of here my love, but may the gods see to it that we meet in the next lifetime."

It wasn't long before both of them were overtaken by a thick layer of ash.

***

The Classroom

Lily Delarosa was overly excited to read about the new Pompeii Artifact exhibit coming to the Timeless Treasures Museum in Youngstown, Ohio in the local newspaper. Her fifth-grade class had recently read a story about the destruction of the famous ancient city in their literature books. *This is just the ticket for my students. I haven't spent the funds yet on a field trip and I know they'd enjoy this one, as I know I will,* she thought as she sipped her morning coffee still in her fluffy robe.

Her heart raced as she drove to work knowing she would get to the office early and hand in the necessary paperwork to her principal to approve the trip and then couldn't wait to share the news with her class.

It was easier than she thought as her request was approved on the spot. Principal Hutchinson had informed her he'd send the paperwork off to the district office that day. "I am proud to say that Willowbrook Academy has more than sufficient funds for this trip and another one in the spring. And I commend you for choosing this fine activity over some of the other frivolous ones I've seen from the other staff members."

Lily blushed and thanked him then headed to her room to get ready for the day. She always enjoyed coming to work in the small private school nestled out in the countryside of Canfield, Ohio. She had been teaching at the private academy for five years now and was looked up to by most of the staff although there were always one or two that seemed to resent her dramatic good looks and air of sophistication that she presented. Her long black hair and pearly white skin made her stand out in a crowd, not to mention the accolades she'd received during her college years.

After uploading all the articles to her Smart Board, she created an assignment for the day involving more research on Pompeii. She rushed to the door as the bell rang to greet her students.

Blaire was the first one in line and not uncommon as she was referred to as the teacher's pet by a few envious ones. The class knew this petite redhead was smart as well as most likely to succeed. "Good morning, Ms. Delarosa. You look pretty today," she said reaching out to hand her a single rose wrapped in a dampened paper towel.

"Why thank you, my dear. How sweet of you. You do know I love roses."

"And art too," added Blaire, smiling to show off her dimples.

Krysten was right behind her with her loaded-down backpack but minus a rose. She and Blaire had been besties since kindergarten.

Bryce, the class clown poked Krysten in the back. "I wonder what that suck up will bring tomorrow?" he pried.

"Shut up! You're just jealous!"

Ms. Delarosa heard the banter and quickly quieted them down as she led them into the classroom. "Now put your things away and take your seats as I have some very exciting news to share!" She clicked on her computer and the Smart Board came to life. The featured article from the newspaper on the Pompeii exhibit came up. Squeals of delight were heard from the students. "We will be able to attend this exhibit in two weeks."

The class cheered and hands were raised with many questions waiting to be answered. Bryce's hand was waving wildly in the air. "Will we see some of those casts of dead people?" His voice was overly excited.

"Not funny!" Blaire called out.

"I'm afraid not, Bryce. It says the event will showcase a few artifacts from the rubble, such as pottery, art, tile fragments, and other items.

Bryce displayed his disappointment by slamming his hand down on his desk.

As soon as all the excitement died down Ms. Delarosa gave instructions for the first few assignments that would have them reading more information on their tablets and taking notes. She was letting them pair up with a buddy and that made the class cheer once again.

Krysten and Blaire had moved their chairs together ready to dive into the assignment, while others took some time deciding who they wanted to pair with.

Krysten had set down her tablet as soon as Ms. Delarosa walked by and turned to her bestie. "You know, I can't figure out why she never married. I mean she's so smart and pretty."

"Well, I think maybe she hasn't found the right one. She's too smart to just settle," Blaire added. "I know I'm never gonna settle."

"We'll see about that," Krysten chuckled.

After lunch, the class was asked to share some of their notes from the morning's assignment. Blaire and Krysten were most eager to share theirs. They had taken notes on how many of the villas in Pompeii were houses to some very wealthy Roman families who even had slaves.

Bryce was not willing to share his notes but Justin, his partner, was more than happy to. He shared his notes on how there were reports of small earthquakes before the actual eruption of Mt. Vesuvius.

After Ms. Delarosa led her class to the front of the school for dismissal, she returned to her room to gather papers and was ready to head home to her small apartment on the other side of town. She decided to pick up her dinner on the way. Being single and living alone gave her no desire to cook. She had planned on reviewing some of the artifacts from the article for the exhibit. *I don't know who's more excited- me or the students*, she thought as she did a deeper dive into the article.

***

The Field Trip

The weather was great the day of the field trip. The sun was out but there was a chill in the air for the beginning of October. The students sauntered into the room as Ms. Delarosa instructed them to keep all of their sweaters and jackets with them. Krysten and Justin's mother also arrived, having signed up to be parent volunteers.

Ms. Delarosa was reading off the names of those who would form into small groups of five. Blaire and Krysten planned to sit together as they were assigned to Krysten's group along with three other students. Bryce was assigned to Justin's mother's group. She was already aware of Bryce's behavior issues after last year's field trip when he was caught picking flowers on exhibit at the state fair.

Principal Hutchinson had popped in to address the class. "Now we all know you have to be on your best behavior, as you do represent Willowbrook. Your teacher has chosen a great exhibit for you so enjoy yourselves and take lots of pictures."

Bryce raised his hand after he heard the word pictures. "So, we are allowed to have our phones on?"

"I believe only during certain times. There will be a docent at the museum, and you will need to turn them off while she is speaking but then I believe you can take pictures after that," Ms. Delarosa said as she began packing sack lunches in a large cooler. The students had planned to have lunch outside on the grounds of the museum which resembled a nature park.

The bus was ready, and everyone walked out front to board. The parent volunteers handed out name tags to each student. It was a thirty-minute ride over to the Timeless Treasures Museum in Youngstown. Before they left the school Ms. Delarosa had reminded them again about proper behavior while looking directly at Bryce as she spoke.

The students cheered as the bus pulled up to the large white brick building with colorful banners hanging from the rooftop announcing the new exhibit. A tall lanky woman in her late fifties greeted them as they exited the bus. "Hello, I am your docent, Ms. Denmore and I will be leading your tour today," she said holding a pile of pamphlets. "I'm sure your teacher has already gone over the rules for the museum."

The students followed in their groups through the large wooden doors and into a long hallway that had several doors that led to various parts of the museum.

"It sure smells musty in here," Krysten whispered to Blaire.

"Well, what did you expect?" Blaire shot back. There are a lot of old dusty artifacts in here. And that makes it even more interesting!"

Krysten just shook her head. *That's my friend. Very smart but always a bit kooky.*

Before they entered the main exhibit Ms. Delarosa scooted alongside Justin's group ready to head off any misbehaviors from Bryce.

Ms. Denmore had instructed the students to come up front as she would give a brief introduction on the destruction of the city as Mount Vesuvius erupted and then prepare to lead them around to all of the artifacts that were encased in glass.

Everyone listened intently to her speech, learning some new things they didn't already know. Ms. Denmore asked if anyone had any questions when she had finished.

Bryce's hand went up and Ms. Delarosa took a deep breath waiting for something unacceptable to pop out of his mouth. "Do you know if any children had survived the destruction?"

Ms.Denmore was quick to respond, "According to historians thousands of the city's inhabitants had fled days prior aware of the many tremors, but we don't have an actual account of what percentage were children."

"So, the ones left were burnt to a crisp?" Bryce asked. "I wish we could see some of these bodies here," he spoke with a gleam in his eyes.

"Some were but it was also the poisonous gases that filled the air as well," Ms. Denmore stated. "And you won't see any of that here. These pieces you are about to see are on loan from a larger museum in London.

Ms. Delarosa jumped in to remind the children that they read about the city frequently having tremors so some unfortunately did ignore it.

The students were ready to follow the docent and begin the tour of the artifacts. Most had their phones out but were instructed not to use a flash setting.

Ms. Denmore had begun to lead the first group over to the first exhibit. "Here you will find a large piece of fresco that was painted on a wall from the House of Cassia, which was a wealthy villa. You can see the cupids depicted here with clouds."

Bryce poked Justin and whispered, "Who cares about seeing these chubby babies."

"Shh!" Justin's mother put up a finger to her lips signaling Bryce to be silent.

As the group moved on to the next exhibit with the volunteer, Blaire's group moved to the first. Ms. Denmore gave her a similar explanation of the remains. Blaire snapped quite a few photos here. "This makes me want to reach out and touch them."

"Well, you'd have to break the glass first, and then we'd be kicked out of here," Krysten said as she eyed the next display.

Each display had a detailed explanation as to what they were viewing, which was enclosed in a glass frame.

Most of the students were interested in the stucco pedestal which had graced a garden from one of the larger villas. It was fully intact and covered in shiny blue mosaic tiles. It was one of the largest pieces in the exhibit. Both parent volunteers took quite a few pictures of this one which they would later post on the school's Facebook page.

As soon as all of the groups had moved on Ms.Denmore informed the students that the most important display was in the next room and they'd have to go one group at a time and be silent as the clay jars were very fragile and any movement could cause them to shatter.

Ms. Delarosa felt butterflies in her stomach hearing about this as she stood right behind the docent at the entrance to the room.

Blaire had approached her teacher with excitement. "Thank you for bringing us here. I'm really enjoying this."

Ms. Delarosa grabbed her hand and smiled. "You are most welcome my dear. This is a once-in-a-lifetime chance to view these items."

Justin's group followed behind the docent as they entered the room. Two large terra cotta jugs were sitting on pedestals behind glass. The group was informed that the first jar was found in the House of Vetti which was owned by another wealthy family. "They loved art and pottery as most of the wealthy class did in Pompeii. The owners were said to have once been slaves but became wealthy through trade. This enabled them to acquire slaves for the villa," Ms. Denmore said.

The students put their hands over their mouths.

"Not too surprising, children," Ms. Denmore said. "It was most common during this time."

Almost all of the students snapped pictures of the jug that was beautifully painted with green and purple ivy vines.

Ms. Delarosa entered along with Krysten's mother and her group. As she moved in closer to the first jug, she felt a rush of adrenaline and her palms became sweaty and clammy. She reached in her purse for a tissue to wipe the sweat off her forehead. She turned around quickly when she heard Bryce's laughter behind her.

"What are you doing here? You're supposed to be back with your group."

"But I wanted to take another picture of this jug," he said as he moved very close to the glass.

Ms.Delarosa went to grab him but became dizzy and had to hold onto the glass to steady herself.

"Are you all right?" Krysten's mother asked, noticing the pallor of the teacher's skin.

"I . . . I'm not sure. Just a bit dizzy."

It wasn't long before she hit the cold tile floor, the contents of her purse spewing about.

"Ms. Delarosa fainted!" Blaire yelled.

Ms. Denmore yelled to one of the volunteers to dial 911 on her cell.

Blaire had rushed to her teacher's side, her pulse racing. "Is she okay? What's wrong?"

"I don't see any blood!" Bryce called out.

Blaire gave him an evil look, "Shut up, you creep!"

The docent had instructed the students to back away. "Seems she's out cold! The paramedics will be here shortly. I need all of you to follow your group out to the lobby area."

***

The Hospital

Lily struggled to open her eyes, which seemed as though they were filled with a liquid cement. Her eyelids felt so heavy. She was able to force one eye open and attempted to use her arm to assist her in lifting the second one, only to find out she was bound down with wires and tubes. *Where the hell am I? What is this place?* She scanned the area with her right eye open to see what appeared to be a hospital room. Being in the hospital a few years back with a kidney infection she knew there was a place on the hospital bed to find a button to call a nurse. Scooting her body slightly upward she pressed the button with the nurse image on it. A loud voice came through a speaker. "Yes, may I help you?"

"Help me? Yes, send someone in here fast!"

It wasn't long before a stalky-built middle-aged nurse came blasting through her door. She headed to the monitors that were above the bed checking all the vitals then read the paper tab that was fastened on Lily's wrist. "Nice to meet you, Miss Lily Delarosa."

"What happened to me?" she asked still struggling with the wires in an attempt to fully sit up.

"You fainted while at the Timeless Treasures Museum. The curator had called 911 and the paramedics brought you in yesterday. You hit your head as well."

"I . . . I don't recall too much of that," Lily spoke shaking her head. "Can you please unhook me?"

"That will be up to the resident physician here. Your vitals seem stable, but he will need to review your reports before he makes that decision," the nurse said as she jotted down something in a folder. "As for that IV- it needs to stay in place. You are severely dehydrated."

"I'm having trouble opening my left eye," Lily said, trying to read the nurse's nametag through her blurry eye. "Can you help me with this, Stella?"

Stella went to the sink and wet a washcloth then dabbed it on Lily's eyes. "This should help, but once they are both fully open, we want you to start drinking some water. It will help your condition."

"Did I have a concussion?"

"No, dear. The scan showed no signs."

Lily took a few gulps of water relieved to hear the news but was still shaken at what happened to land her here. *I do remember being in the room with the artifacts at the museum but nothing more after that. Hmm... and I even had a scan?* "Did you call anyone?"

"Yes, we looked at your medical history when you were here a few years back and the school had also provided us with your emergency information."

"Oh, the school! The school!" Valeria shouted. "What happened to my students?"

Stella took hold of Lily's hand. "Not to worry. I've been told they called in a substitute teacher for the next few days. The nurse's station has received many calls from teachers and a few students checking on your condition."

She sat silent for a moment. "So, who exactly did you call?"

"We called your sister over in Cleveland. She'll be here later this evening."

Just then an attractive tall young doctor walked in holding a clipboard. "Ms. Delarosa, I am Dr. Scott." He stood there staring at the attractive young woman and found himself at a loss for words.

Noticing his silence, Lily held her breath worried as to what the doctor had to say.

She held his glance looking into his deep brown eyes and ones that gave her goosebumps followed by an odd sensation. *This man—there's something about him.*

Coming out of her temporary trance, Lily was able to focus on the doctor's report.

"Looks like all tests are good. Your bloodwork does show a bit of anemia and you are dehydrated. I'd like to keep you here one more day just for observation."

Lily was relieved but was more than ready to go home and back to her students. "I've got to get back to my classroom, doctor. I've got students counting on me."

"I understand but if you go back before you are well rested you won't be doing them any favors."

She bowed her head and nodded.

Dr. Scott went over more instructions for her so she could be discharged tomorrow although Lily was more preoccupied with this man and her mysterious dream.

"And why was I asleep so long having such a vivid nightmare?"

"Most likely due to you being in an unconscious dream state," the dark-haired Doctor replied looking into her pupils with a small flashlight.

Once again Stella experienced another occurrence of goosebumps. As he moved in closer to look at her eyes she sensed a familiarity in his energy.

Stella entered the room again and handed Lily a menu and told her to fill it out as the dietician would be by shortly to pick it up. "You need to eat something. It will help in your healing process. Now I have to finish my rounds and will see you later this evening."

Glancing over the simple menu with three choices for dinner didn't seem to spike up any appetite. But after viewing the choices she selected the chicken soup with pudding for dessert and then set the menu down on her tray.

She felt an odd sensation come over her, one that chilled her to the bone. She was recalling the dream she had. *Was it real? I was running from a volcano!*

The more she focused on the dream, the more all the details came back to her. *How could this be? I mean—I was back in ancient Pompeii. No. Couldn't be!*

She laid her head back on her pillow and closed her eyes trying to recapture her dream. The constant beeping from her monitor was not helping her to relax. She thought about unplugging it but one of the nurses would surely rush in. *I just have to block it out and take some deep breaths.*

Lily felt a bit drowsy. She figured it was from the meds they had given her but she fought the feeling to stay calm and focus on her dream. Bits and pieces had invaded her brain. It was like watching a movie. She retraced her steps along the cobblestone walkway carrying the magnificent jug she was so eager to show off to Marcus and had hopes of it being chosen to grace the halls of the villa. The sun beat down on her bare ivory shoulders. A long black braid hung over her left shoulder.

Seeing her handsome Marcus had her pulse racing as she proudly showed off her prized possession. It was the kiss that melted her heart, but the sudden eruption quickly changed things.

She found herself running through crowds of people as the smoke and ash had reached the city from Mt. Vesuvius. And the little girl who wept in the streets had reached her mother. She also saw the vision of her fleeing with Marcus and trying to head to the boats and then everything got fuzzy. Feeling a choking sensation, she coughed which forced her out of her vision.

Reaching for some water on her side table she took a few sips which seemed to calm her back down. She looked around at her surroundings shaking her head. *It couldn't be. No—there's no way! And Dr. Scott . . . he reminds me so much of Marcus! It had to be a nightmare caused by those meds or I hit my head harder than they thought. And that jug—it was the same one at the museum. This is all too odd.*

Her door opened and her lunch was delivered by an elderly lady in a pink uniform. "Enjoy she said, setting the tray on her side table.

Lily picked at her food, too preoccupied to finish. The visions kept replaying in her head.

Her door opened again, and she was surprised to see Dr. Scott.

"Is something wrong?" Lily asked.

Dr. Scott approached her bedside. "No, not at all Lily. Nurse Stella was getting ready to come check on you, but I told her I'd give her a break and check on you myself."

Lily smiled as she gazed into his warm brown eyes. "I'm glad you did."

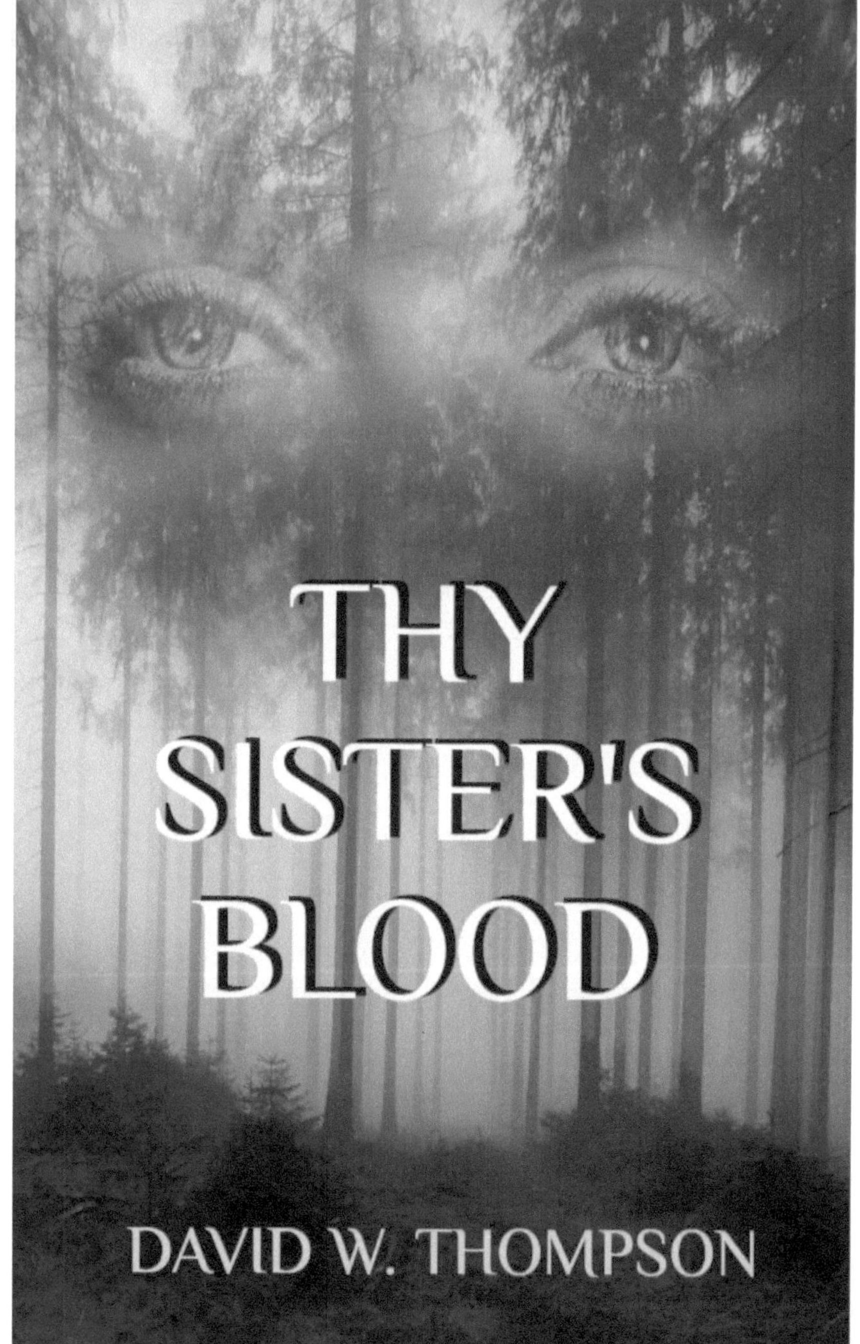

THY
SISTER'S
BLOOD
DAVID W. THOMPSON

Stella Reeves wiped sleep from her eyes and sat up in bed. She frowned at the glowing numbers on her bedside alarm clock: 4:33. Working the mid-shift at the plant, she wasn't accustomed to early morning wakeups. Was the neighbor's cat in heat again? Or was it the sounds of her century old home settling that roused her from her deep dream? A sweet dream it was too…one she was sure to tell her girlfriends about on their trip.

The trip! She did a double-take at the clock and threw off her covers. Her feet hit the cold wooden floors as the phone rang.

"Hello."

"Stella, we're outside waiting for you. We've been ringing the doorbell for five minutes. Did you oversleep again?"

"I'm sorry, Josie. My stupid alarm didn't go off again. Give me five minutes. I'm already packed…just need to dress and I'll be down."

"Hurry up, girl," she snapped. "The river waits for no woman."

The line clicked dead in her hand and Stella dressed hurriedly. She slipped into her new baby blue swimsuit first. Worn jean shorts and a T-shirt advertising her side hustle followed. It read "Stella's Gems and Crystals" with her website emblazoned beneath a purple amethyst. A pair of red, white, and blue water shoes completed her outfit.

She ran a brush through her long hair (a shade often disparaged as dishwater blonde), grabbed her packed river bag, and hustled downstairs.

Thin, raven-haired Josie hopped out of the dark blue SUV's front passenger door and stared down her nose at Stella. She stepped to the back of the vehicle and threw open the back hatch.

"It's about time, Stella. Throw your stuff in back."

Stella tossed in her gear, bit her lip, and climbed into the back seat. *Don't let on she's getting to you, Stella*, she thought.

Rowan, a red-haired woman in her mid-twenties turned in the driver's seat and flashed her bright smile. Stella figured it was that smile that held all the guys in thrall, not her glorious auburn hair as she'd once thought. As lovely as Rowan was, her smile was her best feature, appropriate for someone making their living as a dentist. Everyone gravitated to Rowan, despite her keeping everyone, even Stella, at arm's length.

"Hey, Rowan. Thanks for driving. I've been looking forward to this week since this time last year."

"Yeah, we could tell by how you were waiting for us as planned." Josie said.

"Chill, Josie," Rowan said. "We'll be down county in time to see the sunrise over the water. We won't be dipping our paddles before daylight anyway—when the kayak rental place opens."

"Tell us about the place we're going, Rowan."

"I think you'll like it, Stella. It's a little different than the places we've gone to in past years."

"Different how?"

"Well for one thing, it's the coastal plain, not the mountains. The river is slower, and there's fewer river 'challenges' as Josie calls them. It will be a nice relaxing float. Plus, we should be able to catch a few fish, crabs and maybe an oyster or two to supplement that tasteless dehydrated stuff."

"Yuck, no slimy oysters for me thank you very much." Josie said. "I wipe enough slime out of my kindergartners' noses."

"The joys of being a teacher, huh Josie?"

"Yeah, not so much…"

"Rowan, didn't you say that is where your family's from originally?" Stella asked.

"Sure is, but not that I recall. Not really. We moved away before I started school, but we went back sometimes—when we still had family there."

"Did your dad take you after your mom…" Stella started.

"Yes, he wanted us to know both sides of our family. There aren't many Blackstones left in the area nowadays, but people remember the family name even if it's not for the best of reasons."

"Why is that? Were you a pre-school hoodlum?"

"No, not me, Josie, it was way before my time. There was a colonial ancestor who got herself into a spot of trouble down county."

"What? Wait. I haven't heard of this one. Give it up, Rowan."

"Nope. Sorry, Josie, but that'll be tonight's campfire story…unless you guys are chicken? I know you're not, Stella. Those tales never affect you. Without empirical evidence, you don't believe in anything."

"Wow, is this pick on Stella day? Hey, I'm just realistic, Rowan, but I do get a kick out of a good scary story."

"That usually ends with you in a fit of giggles."

"Well, I like them," Josie said. "Spooky stories around the campfire are a tradition, and if memory serves, it's you who hides in your sleeping bag during the scary ones, Rowan. Remember the guy with the hook for a hand…"

"One time…just one time and I'm branded for life."

***

A brilliant orange and purple sunset greeted their arrival at the campground. The moon was a night or two away from reaching its full phase and its mirror image reflected on the flat surface of the river.

"The tide is still. It's as placid as a lake."

"Like I said, Stella, this trip won't be like our usual float. We'll be putting the kayaks in at the source of a tributary that feeds the Potomac. The locals call it a creek. They'd call it a river where we're from but it's not long enough I guess."

Josie turned her back on the scene and stepped away. "Well, we don't have time to admire the scenery…not if we want to get camp set up before dark. Guess we were too late leaving to enjoy it."

Stella glanced at Rowan and rolled her eyes. "God, what a witch," she breathed.

Rowan smiled but whispered in Stella's ear, "I know, but go easy on her. She just broke up with Jim. Another lesson to not trust people with your heart."

Experience allowed a speedy assemblage of tents. Stella started a small campfire and put water on to boil for hot cocoa. The three women unfolded beach chairs and sat around the fire.

Josie stretched and settled into her chair. "Ok, Rowan, it's story time. Let the tall tales begin."

"Are you sure it won't keep you up tonight?"

"We'll take our chances," Stella laughed.

"Very well. Buckle up, ladies, here goes: As you may know, the Maryland colony was established by folks seeking religious tolerance in the 1630s. Ironically, the colonists were not immune from the witch hysteria that rocked Salem Town. In the late 1600s a woman arrived on these shores who was…different. Her name was Maeve Blackstone. She was…"

"Blackstone? Was she related, Rowan?"

"I'm afraid so, Josie. She was my great-great…I don't remember how many greats— grandmother. She was, by all accounts, a beautiful woman in the prime of her life. No one knows where she came from. She travelled here alone—very unusual for a single woman in that day and age. She didn't get along well with folks. Men were always chasing after her, though she didn't give them the time of day…which spurred them on even more. The local ladies didn't much appreciate the attention she attracted. They claimed she was an 'unnatural' woman, and too prideful and haughty for her 'station.' Maeve traded with the natives and helped those most in need. But mostly she kept to herself, balked at societal norms and avoided colonial functions—including attending church services."

"It sounds like she was an independent woman, not a popular trait in those days."

"Exactly and not now either, Stella. Tensions increased when it became obvious that Maeve was with child. The father was never identified, but every matron in the colony, even while suspecting Maeve's never-do-well hangers on, feared it would be discovered to be their own husband, brother, or son."

"So, they ran her out of town?"

"Let her finish, Stella, but do get on with it, Rowan. I'm ready to hit the sack."

Rowan smiled and continued. "Maeve was used to the townsfolk shunning her, but now they took it to a new level. People whispered curses under their breath when she passed. Children were scolded if they didn't cross the street to avoid her. She became the focal point of church sermons as the preacher railed against godless, immoral, and unnatural acts.

"The colonists' livelihood in those days depended on tobacco farming and fishing. When a drought seized the land, work-worn fingers all pointed at Maeve. Then several children caught what they called the seasoning—likely malaria which was rampant in the area at the time. Hatred towards Maeve grew stronger, and folks began to suggest witchcraft was involved. The icing on the cake was the red tide in the Potomac…"

"Red tide?"

"It's an algae bloom. Hogs and other domestic animals were kept in pens along the creeks allowing the animals to drink, but also fertilizing the water. The drought slowed the waterways to a crawl and algae bloomed at a ferocious rate robbing the water of oxygen. It killed the crabs and thousands of fish floated to the surface, but the scientific explanation wasn't known in the 1600's.

"One brisk autumn day, a young girl breathlessly rushed into the village from the woods. She said she'd heard a baby screaming near Maeve's shack and went to investigate. She claimed Maeve was wading in the creek and mumbling in a strange language. She said she knew Maeve was beseeching Lucifer. That was the final limit. The townspeople held a meeting to decide what was to be done about Maeve. A delegation was nominated to accompany the sheriff the following day to arrest her and bring her to trial.

"When the delegation arrived, they found the door off its hinges and the small windows broken out. Blood stained the ground leading away from the door. Maeve was nowhere to be seen.

"As they investigated, two teenage boys approached from the woods asking for the sheriff. They bragged they'd taken care of the Blackstone witch once and for all. Three of them had knocked on her shack's door at first light. Maeve answered and according to the boys, attacked them without provocation. The oldest, Samuel Breton struck Maeve with a hickory staff. When asked what happened next, the two boys were silent. They scratched their greasy hair, stared blank-eyed at one another, then at the sky and shrugged their shoulders. "I think we hanged her," they answered. "And we don't know what happened to Samuel. He's missing."

"The sheriff asked to be taken to the site of their "deed." Despite the earlier uncertainty, the two boys had no problem retracing their steps. The youngest boy, perhaps fourteen years old, led the way. Rounding a turn in the trail, he fell to his knees and threw up. Gagging on his breakfast, his face flushed, he fought for breath. The sheriff slapped him on the back and the boy pointed down the trail. Samuel Breton swung from a long thick rope dangling from a wide branched oak. The men raced to release him, but it was too late for Samuel. It's said the men never forgot the bulging eyes and purple tongue dangling between his pale lips and I can imagine it to be so.

"The men walked back to town; heads hung low and taking turns carrying the dead lad over their shoulders. Halfway back, the sheriff decided not to punish the two boys. The loss of their friend was enough, but what had become of the witch?

"Back in town, Sophina Bell heard a sound at her door. She sat aside the basket of laundry she was folding and looked out. On her stoop was a baby bundled in a threadbare blanket. Sophina took the babe inside. Attached to the blanket was an envelope containing a note and a wad of bills. The note read:

"Sophina, my sister ye are the only one to treat me with kindness and civility since my arrival on these shores. I can no longer sojourn here, and I implore thee to extend the same kindness to my son. Where I must go is not a fit place for a child. There are ample funds here to provide for him lest Reverend Thomas finds out. Thy family will be forever free from the wrath to come. Our sisterhood is eternal as is my debt to thee. Thy forever sister, Maeve Blackstone.'

"A tremendous thunderstorm and torrential rains tore through the village that night. It laid waste to the crops and blew the roofs off a dozen homes. The river overflowed its banks and washed away the animal pens. Dug water wells were tainted with salt. Three village children were lost to the flood, one being the vomiting fourteen-year-old. The other murderous lad was crushed by a falling timber in his family's barn. Only the family of Sophina Bell were unscathed from the terrors of that night. Theirs were the only crops to make it to harvest that year. Their well remained fresh, a mystery to the town, but not to Sophina. It was many years before the town recovered."

Rowan stood and took a short bow. "And that, ladies, and gentlemen, is the conclusion of tonight's tale. Besides, Josie is tired, right?"

"No, wait. So, what happened to the baby?"

"And Maeve? Did she ever return?"

"The boy, Joshua Blackstone, grew up strong and wise under the tender care of Sophina Bell. He lived to a ripe old age and fathered ten children. The oral tradition says Maeve never returned to town although tales are still told of seeing her floating through the dark woods like a ghost. It's said she's especially active on dark foggy nights and always along the creek after the sun sets. Locals are convinced that dreadful 'accidents' happen to bullies here because of Maeve. To this day, motorists often claim it was the sight of Maeve in the roadway that sent them hurtling off the pavement."

"Do you think the basis of the story is real or just a story the community made up years ago…like a cautionary tale for children?" Josie asked.

"Well, her name is used as a warning to ill-mannered children, but they did name a creek after her. I even have a portrait that's said to be Maeve that my mother had stored in her attic for years. Today, three hundred years later, Maeve is very much alive—one way or another. Anyway, good night, ladies. Sleep thee well. My sleeping bag calls."

***

The day dawned bright and clear after a fitful night's sleep. Rowan was the first one up. A meal of rehydrated scrambled eggs and sausage sat on plates by the fire when the other two poked their heads out of their tents. After breakfast, they broke camp and packed their gear into Rowan's vehicle.

"We should have the river to ourselves today, being a weekday. Don't you think, Rowan?"

"That's my hope, Stella. I think we could all use the peace and quiet. Remember though, we're taking a different route. It will be tomorrow before we reach the river again."

"Yes, a local creek that feeds the Potomac, right? What did you say it was called?"

"I didn't say, Josie. It wouldn't have meant anything to you yesterday. The creek we are floating…well, nobody ever goes on it."

"So, what's it called?"

"Blackstone Creek, named after none other than Maeve Blackstone. It cuts through the middle of her old homestead."

"I guess we know why the superstitious don't go there." Stella stifled a laugh as Rowan turned into the kayak rental area.

"There are more things in heaven and earth, Horatio, than are dreamt of in your philosophy." Rowan quoted.

"Maybe you could go in and quote Shakespeare to Josie's kindergartner class, Rowan?"

"No, Shakespeare was last quarter, Stella." Josie laughed.

"Oh wow, look! The parking lot is full. Everyone and their sister must be kayaking today."

The owner emerged from the shack where the kayak trailer was parked.

"Howdy, young ladies. What can I do for y'all today?"

"Hello," Rowan said as her window slid down. "We have reservations for three kayaks under the name Rowan Blackstone."

"Blackstone? You don't say. I don't reckon any relation to…"

"We'd like to get on the water as soon as possible, sir."

"Yes, ma'am. I'll need y'all to come inside, get your life vests and paddles and ya gotta sign them waivers for me. They just say you won't come after me if you do something stupid and drown yourselves or get eaten by a wild hog."

Stepping inside, the man opened a logbook on his rough cobbled plywood desk.

"Ladies, I think there's been a mistake here though. This here says y'all are wanting to put in on Blackstone Creek. That ain't right, is it?"

"Yes, sir. That's where we're headed."

"You ladies ain't going out there all by your lonesome, are you? You got fellers joining up with you?"

"We'll be fine, sir and I think we're ready now if you are."

"Y'all heard what they say about Blackstone Creek I reckon? Was me, I wouldn't want to be out there after dark. There's something…something that ain't natural haunting that creek."

"Are all these folks out on the river today?" Stella pointed around the parking area.

"No, ma'am. We have a wedding going on. Folks like saying their 'I do's' by the river. Now, how 'bout I take y'all out to the put-in on Roundabout Creek instead of Blackstone. That way I'll be able to sleep tonight."

"I recommend melatonin, sir," Josie said. "We're going to Blackstone Creek."

***

The put-in at Blackstone Creek consisted of a long muddy incline ending at the creek's edge.

The women packed their gear into their kayaks and climbed aboard while the kayak guy watched and picked at his teeth with a sharpened wooden matchstick.

"If y'all keep up a good pace paddling today, you can make the river before dark. There ain't many spots to camp along here anyway and you don't want to spend the night on this creepy creek. Trust me on that."

"Thank you. Sleep well tonight," Josie said.

"Ok then. Y'all have the kayaks rented for the whole week. There's lots of spots on the river to camp and catch some fish. Schools of perch are running up the creeks and river just now. Good luck, have fun and I'll see you purty girls then."

He licked his lips, tipped his hat and turned towards his truck and trailer. As if choreographed, all three women slipped off their shorts and shirts, comfortable now in their swimming suits.

"I didn't think he'd ever leave."

"He was just trying to be helpful, Josie."

"Oh my, I think Mr. Man caught Stella's eye, Rowan. We better keep an eye on her."

"I don't know about you two," Rowan said, "but I really want a nice relaxing float…no pressure. I'm not in a hurry to reach the river or have any concerns about camping on the creek tonight—as long as we can find a flat spot with no cow poop. What do you both think?"

"Sounds like a plan to me."

"Me too."

"Settled then. Let's try the fishing."

They only paddled enough to keep the kayaks moving in a straight line, Rowan caught a bluegill on her first cast and a fat perch on her third. It took Josie a dozen casts before a fifteen-inch largemouth bass snatched her lure. Stella felt all she was doing was beating the water into submission. Cast after cast after cast with no results…not even a nibble. Twice she snagged her lure on underwater obstacles. The first time, she pulled out a two-foot-long branch covered with algae. The second snag snapped her fishing line.

She slapped her rod tip down into the water.

"Easy, Stella," she thought. *"You're here to relax. Chill out."*

She pulled another beetle spin lure from her tackle box and tied it on her line. When she was done, Rowan and Josie had drifted a hundred yards downstream.

"Rowan! Josie?" Neither girl heard her or if so, ignored her.

"No, they wouldn't…" she thought.

She saw a split in the river ahead and thought her luck might improve in that direction. She slipped her phone from its waterproof bag and texted Rowan:

"I'm going to try the right hand split ahead. I'll turn back around and catch up with you two in a bit."

She hit 'send' and tried a cast. Before she'd reeled her lure in, an incoming text from Rowan was received:

"OK, Stell. Don't turn around though. Faster to keep going straight. That split rejoins the main creek in half a mile. I think it's shorter that way though so wait for us if you beat us there."

The fishing was better…much better. Fish after fish succumbed to Stella's deft retrieves. Bass, sunfish, several perches, and a crappie filled out her stringer. A dozen more didn't meet her self-imposed minimum size and were slipped back into the water with care. *I may not be a professional woman like they are, but I'll make tonight's fish fry epic.*

Time slipped away from her. When her arms ached from pulling in fish, she noticed the sun dropping low on the horizon. *No worries, Rowan said this section was only half of a mile long.* She'd done half that already.

She dipped her paddle in the water and pushed herself downstream.

***

"Shouldn't Stella have caught up with us by now? I swear that girl will be late for her own funeral. Has she ever been on time for anything?" Josie asked.

"I'll bet she's caught a ton of fish and lost all track of time. Give her a few minutes. We'll see that blonde head bobbing down the creek any time now."

"Maybe, but I think we should pick a spot and get camp set up anyway. It'll be dark in an hour, ninety minutes at best."

"Ok, I'm sure she'll be here soon. Are you all right with setting up camp over there?" Rowan pointed to a flat sandy spot on the opposite side of the creek.

"Sure. But honestly? After your tale and that weird guy at the kayak place, I'd really rather not be on this creek at all tonight. I'm getting some strange vibes back here. It's giving me the creeps. Don't you feel it?"

Rowan shook her head.

"Maybe I'm a sensitive."

"Ok, Miss Sensitive. Let's put up the tents.

***

Stella paddled until her hands began to cramp. *It can't be much further…can it?* She stopped to get her bearings. She hadn't strayed from her course and hadn't seen any other offshoots in the creek. *Could I have missed one? Was I paddling deeper into the woods…away from my friends?*

Thick fog settled over the creek with unnatural speed and visibility dropped off. Stella remembered the kayak guy talking about strange occurrences in the fog… In front of her, something shook a spicebush at the water's edge. A blurry face appeared— red haired and pale complected. *Rowan!*

"Hey girl! I was worried I'd never catch up with you guys." Rowan pressed her finger to her lips and waded into the water. She was dressed in the fashion of Amish women. A blue top was buttoned to her chin, and her dress ballooned up in the water but would surely reach her ankles. The bonnet on her head allowed only wisps of her red hair to escape.

"What kind of outfit is that and where did you get it?" Stella laughed. "Where's Josie?"

Rowan's lips drew into a straight tight line and her eyes narrowed into slits. Stella stared at her, and her mouth fell open with a new revelation.

"You're…you're not Rowan. Who…?"

The woman seized the side of the kayak and shook it back and forth.

"Stop, you'll capsize me!" Stella pleaded. "I'm not a great swimmer."

The woman reached in and grabbed Stella's wrist in a painful grip.

"T'is not I that would bring harm to thee; thy bloodline ensures that. But tarry not on this day of all days, daughter of Sophina. Return whence thou came."

With a mighty shove, she sent the kayak hurtling backward. Stella's wide brimmed hat flew off her head and disappeared into the water.

Gripping the sides of her small boat, Stella looked up to yell at the woman, but she'd already gone—lost to the mists. As the kayak's backward progress slowed, it turned sideways into the slight current. She laid her paddle across her lap and held her face in her hands.

What just happened to me? she thought. *Am I going crazy? Or is Rowan? It wasn't real…couldn't be. It had to be Rowan…who else? Maeve Blackstone? Yeah, right! I do admire the dedication to their little joke. I'm sure the plot was dreamed up by Josie. Rowan wasn't so cruel… but she did go along with it. We've been best friends for as long as I can remember, sisters of another mother, even though Rowan was afraid to show it. Josie was a newcomer, one Rowan seemed unduly enamored of—another educated woman… unlike me.*

Stella rubbed her eyes and considered turning back, paddling towards the put-in as Rowan (*not Rowan?)* demanded. She could paddle, catch up with them and pretend nothing of consequence happened. No, she had a better idea.

Stella pulled her kayak onto a flat area on the creek bank. She reached into her waterproof bag and pulled out the romance novel she'd brought along. Let them worry about her for a while. It might teach them a lesson about pulling pranks. She yawned and stretched out in the grass and opened her book.

***

A sharp sound snatched her from her dreams. She sat up. *Good, at least it's still daylight. I can catch up with them before dark.*

The rooster crowed again, and Stella's eyes flew wide open. The sun was on the eastern horizon. She'd slept through the night! She set off in her kayak knowing the prankster duo must be nearby. As she navigated a turn in the creek, a flicker of light caught her eye. She craned her neck and yes! It had to be Rowan and Josie. They must be camped at the confluence of the two streams and had a fire started while waiting for her. She attacked the paddles with renewed vigor. Closer and closer she pulled her kayak toward the fire. She felt the burn in her biceps but continued.

"Hey guys! Miss me?" She yelled, but she saw no movement. *They must be in the woods looking for firewood.* She pulled her craft onto the shore in front of the fire. The fog settled in as deep as the night before and she could only discern vague shapes in the distance. *Where are their kayaks?*

Stella climbed out on the bank and headed for the nearby grove of evergreen trees. *There are lots of dead branches on pine trees.*

In short order, Stella had a double armload of dead pine branches. She retraced her steps to return to the fire (and hopefully her friends), when she spotted a small shack.

"Hello? Is anyone home?" There was no answer and she stepped closer. The door was broken loose from its hinges and thrown across the doorway. The windows too were smashed. *Probably a teen vandal's party shack*, she thought.

"Hey, witch. Ye shan't get away. We've got thee now."

Stella jumped but the voice was too far away to be directed at her. It came from the woods to her left, nearer the creek. She headed that way, cautious to make no sound.

She saw the figures ahead of her—three teenage boys and a red-haired woman, all dressed as Rowan (?) was the night before. *Was it Rowan?*

The largest boy smacked a walking stick against the woman's head, and she fell to the forest floor. The other two boys slipped a noose around the woman's neck.

"T'is the end of thy evil sorcery, Maeve Blackstone."

They were really carrying this prank too far!

A movement in the underbrush distracted her from the scene. As the three boys threw the rope over a low hanging oak branch, another figure stepped forward.

"Hold that I might assist thee," the woman said. Like the others, she was dressed in a fashion unknown for centuries. *Is there a historical reenactment happening here? What have I walked into?*

The woman stepped towards the three boys.

"This is naught to do with thee, Sophina Bell. Be on about thy woman's business unless wishing to share this witch's fate."

"Thou art a foolish pup, Samuel Breton." she said. With a flourish, she reached into the pockets of her dress and tossed a fine powder into the boys' faces. They dropped as if boneless and curled at her feet. Sophina removed the noose from the woman's neck and slipped it over Samuel's. She raised both arms to the heavens, her hands balled into fists and snatched them down to her sides.

"Brigid, Máthair, chloisteáil liom! Díoltas! Ceartais!"

The rope pulled against young Samuel's neck and lifted him up and off his feet. He woke and strained against the rope, twisting and pulling…but to no avail. As his worldly concerns ceased, the red-haired woman stirred. Sophina rushed to her side.

"Maeve, ye should flee this place," she said.

"Sophina, my sister. Thank thee. Go back to the village before the others come. The last favor I ask of thee is there." Maeve touched the woman's cheek. "I shan't forget thee."

The woman stood and turned away from her friend. Tears glistened on her cheeks. She looked towards Stella's hiding place. Staring directly into her eyes, Sophina approached her. She pulled an amulet on a leather thong from around her neck and placed it around Stella's.

"Brigid protects thee, but take flight from this place now, daughter. There is no sanctuary for thee here." Sophina turned and ran away through the woods.

***

Josie crawled through the tent opening and saw Rowan stooped over at the water's edge poking at something floating there.

"What are you after, Rowan? Did you drop something in the creek?"

"Stella never showed up last night, Josie. I'm worried about her. Something's wrong." She bent and snatched at what held her interest and pulled it from the water.

"Isn't this Stella's hat?"

"Sweet Jesus, Rowan. I think it is."

"Let's go. Leave camp as it is. We need to go find her now."

***

Two figures stood near the fire when Stella returned. She watched them through the shelter of the trees and fog, hoping they were her friends. But hope didn't make it so. The figures stood between her and where her kayak was beached, leaving little recourse. She sucked in a breath and stepped from the woods into the clearing.

"Who are you men?"

59

The two figures turned towards her and stared. One closed the distance between them and bowed in her direction.

"I am Jedidiah Kirk, sheriff of our king's colony. Ye should worry not who we might be, woman, but thee? Devil spawn, lest I miss my guess. From thine attire, one must assume thee cavort with the Blackstone witch."

The man leapt forward, grabbed her wrist and yanked her towards the fire.

"Wait, Sheriff, I'm not…"

"Let us preserve a modicum of decency, Gideon…" Jedidiah said to the other man and nodded towards the fire.

Gideon snatched a blanket and tossed it at Stella. "Cover thyself, witch!"

Jedidiah nodded uphill away from the trees and Gideon sprinted off in that direction.

"Come, witch."

Stella was dragged along in the direction Gideon ran. She pulled against the sheriff, but his grip was strong. Her fingers tingled as if a hundred tiny needles pricked at her flesh. She twisted and dragged her feet in the sandy soil, cursing him when all else failed.

"Thy devil's tongue shan't serve thee well here, witch."

When they crested the hill, a rustic village spread out before them in the valley below.

"What is that? Is it a movie set? You're all actors, aren't you? You need to turn me loose, Jedidiah or whatever your name is. I'm not part of this."

"I know not of what thee speak, witch. Hold thy tongue lest I remove it."

"Witch! Witch! We've captured one of the witches!" echoed Gideon's voice from below.

Through a settling fog, Stella saw the scramble of figures below. Many carried pitchforks, shovels, rakes or hatchets. All were dressed in period clothes.

"A warm reception awaits thee," the sheriff said.

Stella felt a warmth settle between her breasts and touched Sophina's amulet with her free hand. She pulled it off and swiped it at the Sheriff's face and again at his restraining hand. A bloody line appeared across his cheek, just under his eye. Stella felt his grip lessen and she snatched her hand away.

***

"I don't remember this fork in the creek being so long. I would've thought we'd be back to where it split off by now."

"We should be, Rowan. Do you notice anything odd?"

"Only that my arms are getting worn out from paddling."

"Look ahead, around that next bend? That bank of fog has been getting thicker by the minute, yet we don't seem to be getting any closer to it. I swear we were this far away from it a half hour ago."

Rowan stopped paddling and looked around.

"I see what you're saying. Look over there." Rowan pointed to a rusted antique milk can stuck in the vines at the water's edge. "I noticed that can twenty minutes ago."

"What is happening?"

"There must be an undercurrent. We need to paddle faster. I feel it in my bones, Stella is in trouble. I know it now."

***

Stella ran as if the devil was chasing her, the reality being not much better. Thorns pierced her thin water shoes and rocks bruised her heels, but the sound of footfalls behind her spurred her on.

As she crested the hill above the town, she saw her salvation in the form of the small yellow kayak waiting below. She continued at the

61

same speed…too fast for her descent. She stumbled over her own feet and face-planted in the dirt. A darkened world swirled around her.

"I have you now, witch," then "humph" as the sheriff hit the ground behind her with a thud. Stella turned to see a ghostly female figure pointing to the creek. "Hurry, daughter."

As she ran, seconds became minutes and the minutes, hours. *I don't recall reading about an eclipse today, she thought. Or was the darkness a symptom of a concussion? Surely, I didn't land that hard.*

Drawing near the creek's edge, she hazarded a glance over her shoulder. Were all the demons of hell pursuing her…? Townspeople, armed to the teeth, screaming and brandishing their weapons, flowed over the hill towards her, and the wall of fog followed them.

She leapt into her kayak with the dexterity of a Western movie star mounting his steed. Her paddle slipped into her hands as if an extension of herself.

The sky darkened as the fog thickened. Tendrils grasping like hooked fingers, clawing, pulling her into their dark embrace. The sound of talons scratching against the sides of her boat, and she paddled, long powerful strokes that barely edged her forward.

The first of the colonists reached the water and waded in. *How can they move along that muddy bottom faster than I can paddle?*

Stroke after stroke she paddled against unseen restraints as the enraged horde gained on her. Fearful of losing even one stroke, she rubbed against the amulet with her chin. *Sophina, help me. Maeve, do you remember your promise?*

***

"Look Josie, does it look like the fog is thinning ahead?"

"I can't tell for sure…maybe a little? We do seem to be moving forward now at least. Your milk can has fallen behind us."

"Ok, keep your eyes peeled for her yellow kayak. We should be able to spot it even through this hellish fog."

"The fog might be the least of our worries, Rowan. As dark as it's getting, I think we're in for a nasty storm. We need to find shelter ourselves."

"I'm afraid you're right about the storm, and I understand if you need to turn back, but I'm going after Stella. I don't know what I'd do if anything happened to her."

"You can't help her if you're swept away in a storm or get flipped over trying to navigate in the dark. I can't see ten feet in front of me now."

"Hell, or high water, I have to be there if she needs me."

***

Stella turned her kayak toward the center of the creek, where the wall of fog thinned. Disembodied voices whispered in her ears:

"Return to face thy crimes, witch."

"Thou cannot escape thy fate."

"Thy atonement is at hand."

"Denounce the dark lord that thou might escape perdition."

Stella ignored them all. Her arms ached and a sharp pain stabbed her between her shoulder blades. Rain slapped against her face, and a shiver ran through her body as a warmth spread through her chest emanating from her amulet.

Stella lurched forward as her kayak jerked to a stop. *Have I hit a rock or a fallen tree? Too dark to see.* She heard rather than saw the wrinkled clawed hands creep over the side...scratching and clawing their way towards her. Splashes in the water, vague figures pulling her back, snatching her paddle…

"Kill the Witch. Death to the Witch," the darkness whispered.

Stella yanked the paddle free and swung it blindly around the kayak. Left, then right, but her attackers were untouched. Her efforts

63

only slapped the water. Again, she swung a roundhouse blow and over the side she went, the creek water rising to meet her.

Unseen hands snatched at her legs, drawing her down into the depths. *This can't be. The creek isn't so deep.*

She kicked out with both feet, lost one water shoe to a grasping hand and for a moment, was free. But her attackers were not to be denied. Clawing at her ankles, her arms subdued, they pulled her down and down…and down…

***

"Stella!"

She heard the voice but couldn't determine its source. The woman in the other kayak slid across the water toward her. Her herculean effort sending up a watery rooster tail in its wake.

Stella saw the boat's approach through the water as if in a dream.

"Maeve, you've come to save me."

She saw the red hair streaming in the water above her…a hand reaching out to pull her from her watery grave. She snatched it.

"Stella! Stella, thank God!" She welcomed the embrace of the woman's strong arms—comforting, familiar…

Rowan. Sister.

***

Josie was standing at the water's edge as they rounded the last bend. She waded into the shallows to greet them, waving Stella's water shoe in the air.

"Hey girl, did you lose something? Where was she, Rowan? Are you ok, Stella? What happened?"

The two women beached their crafts and fell onto the sand.

"It is a long story I'll save for our next campfire. Suffice to say I took a break and fell asleep for a bit."

64

"I knew it. I told Rowan you fell asleep, but she texted you dozens of times and yelled for you half the night. She was worried and didn't sleep a wink, but I knew you were Ok."

Stella caught Rowan's gaze and shook her head. "Don't," she mouthed.

"Hey, where did you get that? Is it a new necklace?"

"Unless I'm mistaken," Rowan said. "that's Brigid's cross. It's kind of a protection talisman for folks of Irish descent. I've only seen one with the yellow gem forming the center square though."

"Where did you see it, Rowan?"

"Maeve is wearing one like it in the portrait my mother gave me, Josie. Unique. I'll bet the stone has a special meaning too. Right, Stella?"

"It does, Rowan. Topaz is the gem that symbolizes fidelity, loyalty and friendship."

"I love it. Where can I get one like it?"

"It's a gift that I'll always treasure, Josie, but you don't want to go through what I did to get it."

"One thing for sure, we won't forget this trip for a while," Josie said.

"You don't know half of it," Stella said.

"You know what? Let's have a toast." Rowan raised her arm high.

They grasped hands. Stella smiled, seeing two spectral figures appear to join theirs to form a single fist. Raising it high into the air, they shook their knotted hands.

"Sisters forever?"

"Sisters forever!"

The river and three kayaks beckoned them, and their next adventure awaited.

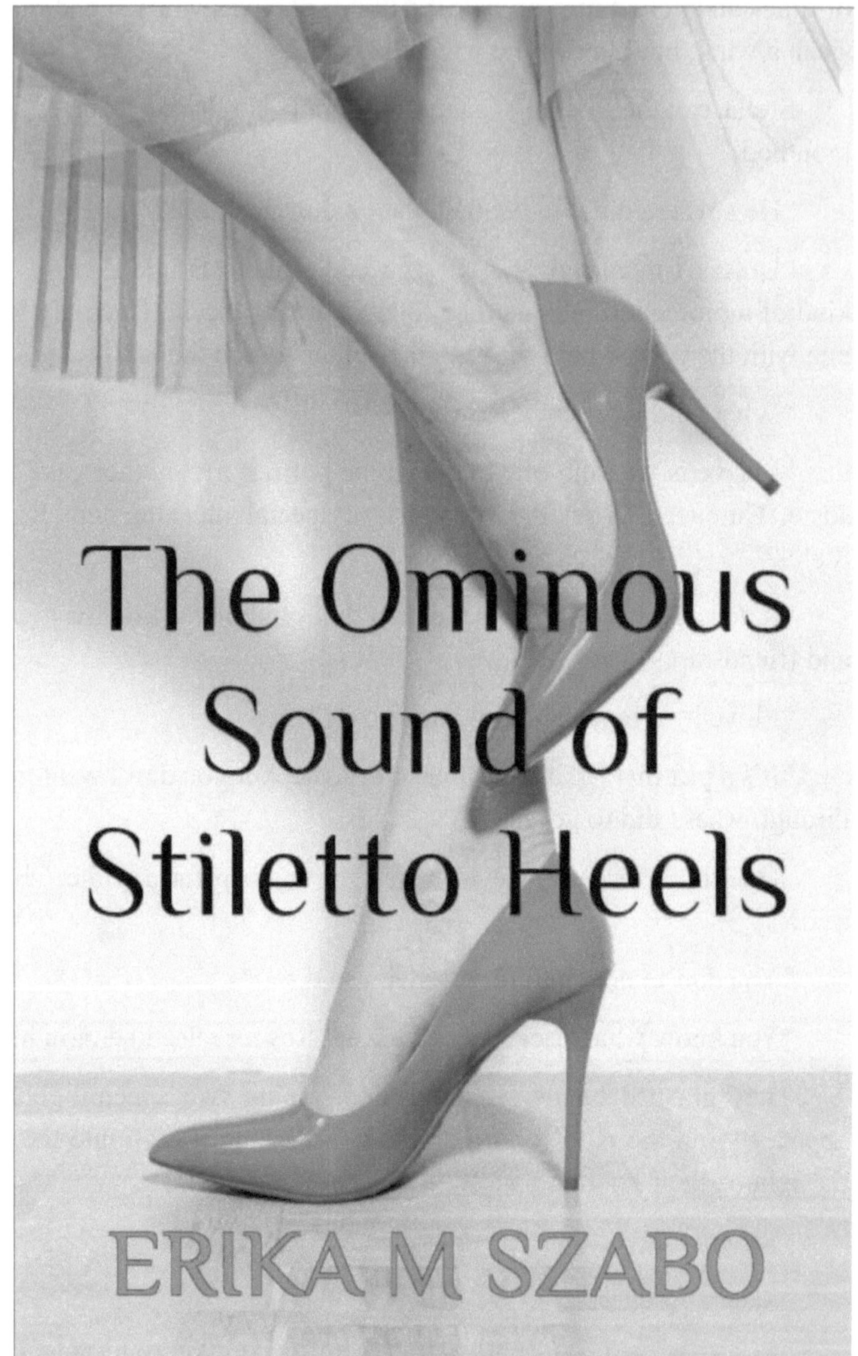
The Ominous
Sound of
Stiletto Heels
ERIKA M SZABO

Sara, a sixteen-year-old brunette with an athletic physique, was a new student at Hillcrest Boarding School. She was unhappy to leave her friends behind, but her father insisted on moving her to a more prestigious school. "The last two years are most critical before continuing your education," he said. "And Hillcrest is the finest. Nearly all of their students get into reputable universities."

Her parents were impressed by Madame Chloe, the school principal, especially her mother who embraced her role as a socialite in high society circles. At their meeting, Madame Chloe dressed impeccably in expensive and fashionable name-brand outfits, and the way she presented herself and the school's achievements instantly won them over.

At first, Sara found the principal charming as well. However, as the conversation progressed, the way Madame Chloe's eyes darted to her and scanned her entire body, made her uncomfortable. Despite the flashing of those dark brown eyes only lasting for a split second, Sara sensed something sinister behind the pleasant exterior of the woman's lovely smile, pristine clothes, manicured nails, and flawless hairstyle.

Sara always listened to her gut feelings and begged her parents not to make her change schools, but her parents, visibly mesmerized by the principal's performance, made their final decision despite Sara's weak objections. "You know nothing about life! Gut feelings are not reliable," her mother shouted. "The school's reputation is impeccable. You're going to be a student there, and that's final."

Sara gave in and hesitantly accepted her parents' decision and moved into her new school's dorm at Hillcrest. Knowing that every school has its social hierarchy, she thought she would need some time to fit in and catch up. However, it soon became apparent that this school was different from others.

There was no hierarchy among teachers or students. There were subordinates and only one top dog: the principal and history professor, Madame Chloe. Her authority and dominance were obvious as she walked in her signature bright red stiletto-heel shoes, her cold eyes darting from student to student. The sound of those heels in the hallways would quiet the students and even the fellow teachers. When she walked past, a chill filled the air. Her presence commanded fear and obedience from everyone around her. Sara couldn't help but wonder what it must be like to have that kind of authority and influence over so many people.

Madame Chloe ruled with an iron fist and Sara soon heard rumors that her physical fist brutally broke several bones over the years. Students had no one to report the physical abuse to, and unfortunately, by the time they were allowed to see their parents, their injuries had healed. Because of the school's reputation and the highly respected principal's words against the students, people dismissed the complaints as childish rumors. The injured students had no proof.

Although Sara had a hard time keeping her rebellious nature under control, she kept quiet while keeping her eyes and ears open. Until… about two weeks into the school year, she stood by her locker across from Madame Chloe's office when she saw her classmate, a petite blonde girl staggering out of the room. Vera sobbed pressing her hand to her side, visibly in pain.

Sara followed her into the bathroom, where two girls stood by the sink and hugged the crying girl.

"You'll be alright," Kate, a dark-skinned statuesque girl whispered, wiping Vera's tears.

"I can't take it anymore!" Vera cried. "This was the third time this week and she didn't even tell me why I deserved such a harsh punishment. My leg is still bruised where she kicked me two days ago." She rolled down her knee-high socks. She gasped and stood up, her face contorting in pain. She held her side. "I think she broke my ribs this time," she sobbed.

Mary, a plump redhead, huffed. "She's a cruel sadist! She yanked my hair so hard yesterday that she pulled out a strand and my scalp bled all afternoon. All because when the monster said, 'eyes on your books' I looked at Vera."

"Why doesn't anyone do something about this?" Sara asked, closely watching the group's reaction.

"What can we do? We can't prove anything," Kate shrugged despairingly, tears flowing down her cheeks. "Nobody believes us, not even our parents."

"What about the teachers?" Sara questioned.

Mary shook her curly hair. "They know what's happening but are too scared to say anything. The only teacher who was brave enough to gather evidence against this monster disappeared before you got here."

"What do you mean by disappeared? Did she leave school?" Sara asked. The three girls seemed to sense Sarah's authoritative yet compassionate nature and opened up.

"Oh, no," Kate shivered and said, "Miss Clara was in my room that night, taking pictures of my bruised ribs and listened to the tape I recorded on the small device she gave me. I hid the recorder in my underwear and turned it on when I was ordered to Madame Chloe's room. She beat me so badly that day... the more I screamed and begged her to stop, the more she hit me. Just remembering her face, how much she enjoyed watching me wiggle in pain, and the obscenities coming out of her painted mouth, makes me nauseous."

"We never saw Miss Clara again and those who dared to ask either were ignored by the teachers or got a severe beating from that red shoe monster," Mary added. "I swear I'm never going to wear red shoes as long as I live."

"Does she treat every student like this?" Sara asked.

"Oh, no!" Vera sighed. "She picks her targets very carefully, and the three of us are the ones who take the brunt of her punishment."

"What do you mean by that?"

"We all come from poor, broken families, and the only way we could be students here is because we're exceptionally smart. We were picked in our old schools by "Good Samaritan" rich sponsors who paid our tuition that we would pay back with loyalty and dedicated work later," Kate whispered with tears in her eyes, but Sara sensed sarcasm behind her words. "My mother is so blinded by the opportunity she never had that no matter what I tell her about the abuse, she finds excuses and shuts me up. 'Just keep quiet. It's for your future' she always says."

"That's terrible!" Sara cried out. "She should listen to you and protect you."

"Easy for you to say!" Vera snapped. "My mother is just a lowly cleaning woman and not a duchess like yours. Nobody would believe her if she complained to the authorities. And if she took me home, without my sponsor's money, I wouldn't have the opportunity to get a high-quality education. That monster knows exactly who to pick to live out her sick fantasies on. She never picks kids from influential, rich families."

"I'm so sorry! We can't let her get away with this. We must stop that pervert!" Sarah scanned the girls' faces.

"And why would you help us?" Mary asked with doubt in her voice.

"Nobody should be treated like this!" Sara angrily replied. "You're all smarter and more talented than me. You shouldn't have to suffer for the education my parents' money can easily pay for."

The group stared at Sara with hope in their eyes when the bell rang. "Okay, let's get back to class and play the role of the most diligent and most obedient student. Tell me everything you know when we have a chance to talk again in private, and we'll come up with a plan to stop her. When we have enough evidence, I'll talk to my Godfather. His law firm is the biggest and most influential in the country."

The trio listened to Sara with hopeful smiles. Kate said, "The best place to talk privately is the library because nobody spends time there lately unless they really have to. It stinks there and nobody knows why," Kate said, wrinkling her nose.

Everyone agreed and the next day during the long recess they met in the library. They chose a secluded corner where nobody could overhear them. "It stinks here," Mary grimaced. "No wonder we're the only ones here."

The four girls sat close to each other. "I don't care about the smell," Sara whispered. "At least we can talk without anybody disturbing us. What do you know about Miss Clara's disappearance? Did anyone see her after she left Kate's room?" She asked.

Vera whispered back, "A girl in my French class told me that she saw Madame Chloe and Miss Clara walking down the hall late at night when she was coming back from the bathroom. She wondered what they were doing in the dorm building so late. She considered following them but was too scared to be seen by the principal, so she closed the door."

"Did anyone see Miss Clara after that?" Sara asked.

"We asked the teachers and a lot of students, but nobody saw her after that night," Kate replied anxiously wringing her fingers.

"So, they walked together, and nobody ever saw Miss Clara again," Sara speculated. "I assume the monster didn't offer any explanation, or did she?"

"Of course not!" Mary huffed. "And nobody dared to ask her."

"Shh!" Sara hushed the others and looked at the librarian and a short, balding man in a janitor uniform. He was walking toward the window at the far side of the large room with disgusted looks on their faces.

"Phew!" Mr. Smith exclaimed. "You were right, Miss Rose. It still stinks here."

"You must do something about it! It smells like a dead rat or rather an army of dead rats," the tall, bony woman whose face resembled a horse exclaimed.

"Miss, I have searched the library many times over the past two weeks and have not found any dead animals." What else can I do?"

"Search again!" the woman ordered.

The janitor threw his arms up in desperation, turned, and walked away from the librarian.

Sara watched him as he walked toward the door, sneaking a side glance at the girls sitting in the corner. "My intuition tells me he knows something," Sara whispered. "We have to talk to that man." She stood up and hurried toward the door trailed by the three girls.

They caught up with the janitor in the hallway leading to the classrooms. "Mr. Smith," Sara called out to the man walking in deep thought.

"Yes, Miss," he turned toward Sara and scanned the group walking behind her.

"Can we talk to you?" Sara asked.

The janitor seemed surprised. "Yes, Miss." But his eyes anxiously locked on the principal's door. "But not here," he muttered. "If Madame Chloe saw me talking to students, I'd be in big trouble. You can find me in the maintenance room in the basement after dinner." He said and hurried away.

They spent the rest of the day trying not to draw the principal's attention to themselves. After dinner when the hallways were empty, they tiptoed toward the basement door. "What if the monster caught us?" Sara asked.

"Oh, everybody knows that after dinner she locks herself in her room and watches sadist porn movies. She never comes out of her room before ten to shut off the lights." Mary said in disgust.

"How do you know?"

"Miss Clara told us. That was the only time she dared to come to our rooms to gather proof against the monster."

They opened the basement door and crept down the steps. The warm musty air tickled their noses with the heavy smell of chemicals. The janitor waited for them and ushered them into the maintenance room. Sara decided to tell him everything they knew. She assured him that if he knew anything about the abuse and disappearance of Miss Clara, even the smallest detail. "My uncle is the Chief of Police," Sara assured the janitor. "If we could provide him with solid proof and information, I'm sure he would close the school and start an investigation. And my godfather's law firm would surely protect you."

"I believe you, Miss. Your family's ties are stronger and higher than Madame Chloe's, so when it comes to that, I know they would protect me," Mr. Smith nodded. "I know things, but I've been afraid to tell anyone. People who dare to say anything and Madame Chloe finds out who the whistleblower is, they vanish."

"If you feel uncomfortable, you don't even need to tell us what you know. Just tell me you have solid proof and I'll set up a meeting with my uncle."

The janitor sighed and with a determined look on his face started talking. "I know the way she's treated some of the students. She's a sick woman. Miss Clara told me and gave me some pictures to keep them safe. But we didn't know who to trust. Two years ago, another teacher gathered enough proof and reported it to a lieutenant at the station. She disappeared the next day and the evidence vanished with her."

The three girls looked at each other. "Miss Antoinette," Mary whispered. "She was my favorite teacher."

Mr. Smith nodded. "Nobody knew what had happened to her, but a week after Miss Clara's sudden disappearance, the awful smell in the library made me remember something. Back then the smell of decay lingered for months, and we never found out where it came from. But yesterday, after I talked to the librarian, I got the school building blueprint from the secretary. I noticed that there is a room right under the library in the basement that I'd never seen. I measured the distance from the boiler room and there was nothing there but a brick wall at the end of the hallway where the blueprint indicates a small room. But when I carefully looked at every inch of the wall, I found a keyhole and some brick dust underneath it on the floor."

"That must be a hidden door!" Sara shouted.

"That's what I think, and the smell is strongest there."

"Do you… do you think Miss Clara is there… dead?" Kate cried out.

"After thinking things over, I'm afraid so, Miss."

Sara shivered. "We must find the key and look inside. But where could it be?"

"I'm almost certain Madame Chloe has the key," the janitor said. "The night Miss Clara disappeared I was working late. When I finished around 2 am and stepped out into the hallway, I saw Madame Chloe walking up the steps barefoot. I wondered what she was doing in the basement in the middle of the night and why she wasn't wearing those awful red shoes."

"That's it! We have to find that key in the principal's office," Sara decided.

"But how? She always locks the door when she's not in the office," Mary objected.

Mr. Smith raised his hand to quiet the girls. "No need for that!" he said calmly. "I just made a wax impression of the keyhole and tonight I'll make a copy of the key from the impression. Meet me here tomorrow night and I'll tell you what I found in that room. Now go back to your rooms but be careful."

Sleep avoided the girls all night and the next day dragged on. Finally, after dinner when the halls quieted down and the students retreated into their rooms to study, the four friends tiptoed to the basement door and hurried down the stairs. Mr. Smith awaited them sitting on the bench with a dire expression on his face and his shoulders slumped.

"What did you find?" Sara asked.

"I… I found both of them," he cried out. "Poor Miss Antoinette and poor Miss Clara!" He sobbed.

"Are they both…" Kate didn't finish.

"Yes, Miss. Both are dead."

***

The following morning, Sara sought permission to call her father. Switching to French—a language unbeknownst to the eavesdropping secretary who monitored all student calls—she recounted every harrowing detail, from their eerie findings to the grim discovery of lifeless bodies hidden in the basement. Her voice trembled as she spoke, yet she conveyed each word with precision.

"Hold on and don't say anything to anyone," her father instructed after absorbing the gravity of her revelations. "I'll handle everything. We'll arrive with your uncle and a team of detectives as swiftly as possible."

During the bustling lunch hour, the previously tranquil corridors of Hillcrest School were now a hive of activity, teeming with policemen and detectives. They converged upon the building like ants for a picnic, driven by their urgent purpose. The atmosphere was charged with tension, palpable in every corner as students and teachers clustered together in the dining room, exchanging hushed whispers filled with anxiety and speculation.

Without warning, the dining room door slammed shut, and the sharp clatter of locks clicking reverberated through the room, sending a shiver down everyone's spine. The atmosphere grew tense as they were summoned one by one into a cramped side room for intense interrogation. As the hours dragged on, a heavy mountain of evidence and damning testimonies piled up against Madame Chloe. She stood accused of heinous crimes – the brutal abuse of children and the cold-blooded murder of two innocent souls.

The once intimidating figure of Madame Chloe was now a mere shell, being led away in handcuffs by the authorities. News of her downfall spread like wildfire through Hillcrest School, bringing with it a sense of relief. The oppressive atmosphere that once hung over the school, fueled by fear and uncertainty at the sound of red stiletto heels clicking down the halls, was now lifted. Justice had been served and peace could finally be restored.

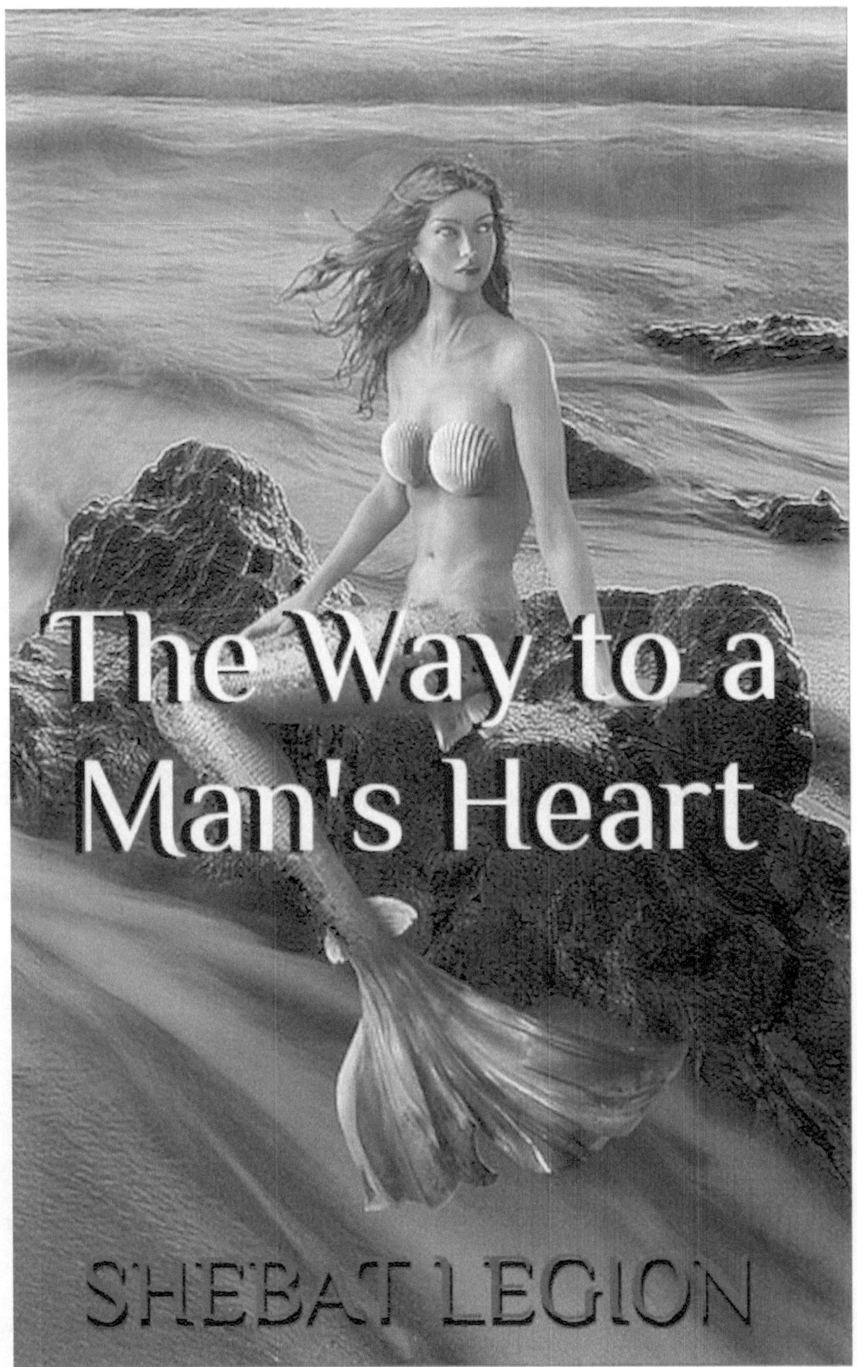

The Way to a
Man's Heart

SHEBAT LEGION

The Siren sang, and the struggling man was held fast to the chair as if bound in chains.

"You can't say this is the prelude," she mused. She looked at the man, who stared back at her, paralyzed. "And the acoustics are not the best."

She cleared her throat and smiled, baring pointed teeth.

"There is a saying that the way to a man's heart is through his stomach. There is much truth to this. Of course, you probably mean something different than I do, but the expression stands."

The man grunted frantically.

"There are many ways to a man's heart. For example, smashing my way through the chest does the trick if I feel snarly."

The Siren gave the man a playful poke.

"The stomach is soft. See?" She poked him again, "Easy access to the heart before it becomes my evening meal."

The man gurgled, and the Siren cocked a dainty ear.

"What am I? Well, I've been called many things! But what I really am is a Siren."

The man grunted again, looking at the Siren's legs.

"Oh, these?" The Siren posed, one leg outstretched, toe pointed. "A little razzle-dazzle. A spell, a little sleight of hand."

"Mmph?"

"How did you get here? I sang that song at the bar. Remember? No? Well, men like you hear what they want to hear."

The man strained against his invisible restraint, and the Siren trilled a clear note, rendering him helpless.

"Men like you," the Siren spat. "Your first words to me were, 'hey, sexy.' You had a shine in your eyes—the shine of a predator, and I should know."

"Mmph!!"

"Okay. I'll wait. By all means, continue. Let's have a chat. Let's get to know each other. Isn't that what you wanted? I'm just kidding; we both know what you wanted."

"Mmph, mmph!"

"I am a carnivore, but what I like to feed on is fear, an important distinction." The Siren added, almost sheepishly, "Call it a quirk, a fetish maybe." She shrugged. "So, if you want to chit-chat, just calm down, and we can prolong things for a bit, but then I really must get to it. So, I was saying. Blood is all well and good, but fear is the real deal. Blood without fear is like a hamburger without the French fries, the caviar without the champagne. Blood without fear is just missing, you know? Incomplete, leaving me hungry, as if I fed on grass."

The man gave a groan and a mumble, and the Siren cocked her head, pondering the question.

"Do I ever feel guilty? You ask the strangest questions. Think of what I do as performing a service. Would you ask the electrician who upgrades your wiring if he felt guilty for removing the faulty cable?

The man stared.

"I can see this idea holds some interest for you. Is that my purpose, you wonder, to remove the faulty people, the evildoer? The short answer is no. The long answer is that there is no such thing as a human that isn't faulty."

The man struggled again; his breath labored.

"Don't run. You started this. I knew you would. I even laid a bet on it. As soon as I sang my little song, I said, "Joe, that's my guy. Who's Joe? Doesn't matter. And I dressed for the occasion." The Siren twirled, and the green sequins on her gown shimmered beneath the muted hotel room ceiling light. "Isn't this dress to die for? And it was on sale!"

The man whined desperately.

"Why you? Ha, you might ask. So, I sit there with a mocktail and wait for men like you, who like to take off their wedding rings and start feeding me lines like someone feeding bread to a pigeon."

A tear slid down the man's cheek.

"But you know, you are special. No, really. It didn't take long before you asked me to have dinner in your room. But unfortunately, you didn't specify what was on the menu, so you only have yourself to blame."

The man whimpered.

"No, don't beg. Or do. It won't change anything, but hey, free will and all that. You do you."

The man wept.

"And now you are crying. Would you like a drink before we get to things? What's your poison again? Scotch? Funny, I would have taken you for a martini kind of guy. Oh, come on. I'm funny; you have to admit it. No, really. You have to."

"Mmph!"

"Because I say so."

"Mmph!"

"Because I'm in charge here."

The Siren sang a brief aria, and the man's hand was free to accept his drink, which he threw back suddenly, gulping the scotch, then gasping.

"Don't," he managed.

"Arguing with me isn't going to change anything. But I am feeling a trifle loquacious. And I tend to play with my food, a bad habit. So. What do you do for a living? Let me guess; let me think. You are a sales manager. No? Communications? No? Computers? No? Wow, I'm rarely this off."

"Please," he began to sob.

"Oh, come on, lighten up. Want another drink?"

The Siren hummed as she poured.

"There you go, better? Better for you anyway. You can't hold your drink, that's for sure. Remember when I said fear is the thing? Yes, you are fearful. But blurry and intoxicated? That won't do."

The man screamed.

"That's better. Yes, I know it hurts."

The man groped one-handed into his pocket and pulled out his wallet, dropping it hastily.

"No, I don't want to see pictures of your kids, or why not? Cute. Is that your wife? Now, see? She looks like a nice woman. Do you want to call her? No, really. Tell me, what would you say to her if you could? Would you say you were sorry? This picture doesn't show the black eye you gave her."

The man started.

"Of course, I know."

"Didn't," he mumbled.

"You didn't mean it? What did you mean, then? What else could you have meant except for a variation of what I am doing to you right now? Power to do, power to hurt, power to scare. Power to kill."

"What…"

"What do you mean, what do I mean? So, you think you weren't killing a part of her every time you hit her, every time you scared her enough to try to escape with the kids, but she didn't get very far because she doesn't think she has an escape? Because wherever she goes, there you are? You are just as much of a monster as I am."

The Siren crossed her arms and glared.

"Let's just get on with it. Your excuse-making is leaving a bad taste in my mouth, and I haven't even started on the hors-d'oeuvres yet."

"Ahh!"

"That hurt? I bet it did. I won't say I'm sorry; I always enjoyed liver pate."

"No!"

"Yes, scream. She did, didn't she? Until she didn't. She kept silent with her hands in front of her face as if that could somehow hide from you. Scream away."

The man wept.

"Ah, there it is. You. Are. Sorry. Did she say that too? Even if she didn't know why? Sure, she did."

The Siren sang a discordant note, and the man, suddenly able to move, stumbled away, bleeding.

"Where do you think you are going?" The Siren chuckled. "Think you can make it to the door? Let me see you try. Come on, you cowardly filth of a human sack of entrails, I will give you a head start. One, two, three, got you! Want to try again? I will cover my eyes this time. One, two..."

The man fell to the floor, screaming.

"That was too easy; I'm disappointed, a tough guy like you. What are you, six-foot-something? Your wife is what, five-foot something? I have one last thing to say, and then I am done."

The man curled into a ball, shivering.

"You should be thanking me. Your family is better off without you. I hope she has insurance. I hope she goes on to have a better life. I hope she spits on your grave. She may not; I have no control over that, but I wish her the best, just the same."

The man closed his eyes, weeping helplessly.

"Siren, human, it's all the same in the end. Women have to have each other's back. I like to think she would thank me if she knew. Or maybe she would feel sorry for you; it's hard to say. But I know she feared you enough to get my attention. I heard her, loud and clear."

The man took a deep breath, and his muscles tensed in preparation.

"So, here I am. I guess you could call me your fate. Sure. I like that. A monster by any other name is still a monster."

The Siren gave the man a sudden kick.

"Oh, come on, where's your sense of humor?"

In one last desperate attempt, the man launched at the Siren, who laughed in delight, "That's it. Take it like a man. Fight back. Come on. No? Can't? She couldn't either."

The man trembled.

"Just goes to show what goes around, comes around."

The man gasped for air.

"Sometimes."

The man wailed, then lay quiet.

"Oh, that fear, let me tell you, nobody will ever fear you again."

The Siren checked and then chuckled again, prodding the corpse with the tip of her shoe, and then she began to feed. Afterward, she gave a delicate burp and entered the luxurious hotel bathroom. She tossed a patchouli-scented bath bomb into the tub as it filled with hot water, easing herself into the whirlpool and turning on the jets. Then, with a quick whispered spell, she shucked her land legs, stretched out her flippers, and sighed, contented, sated, and above all else, vindicated.

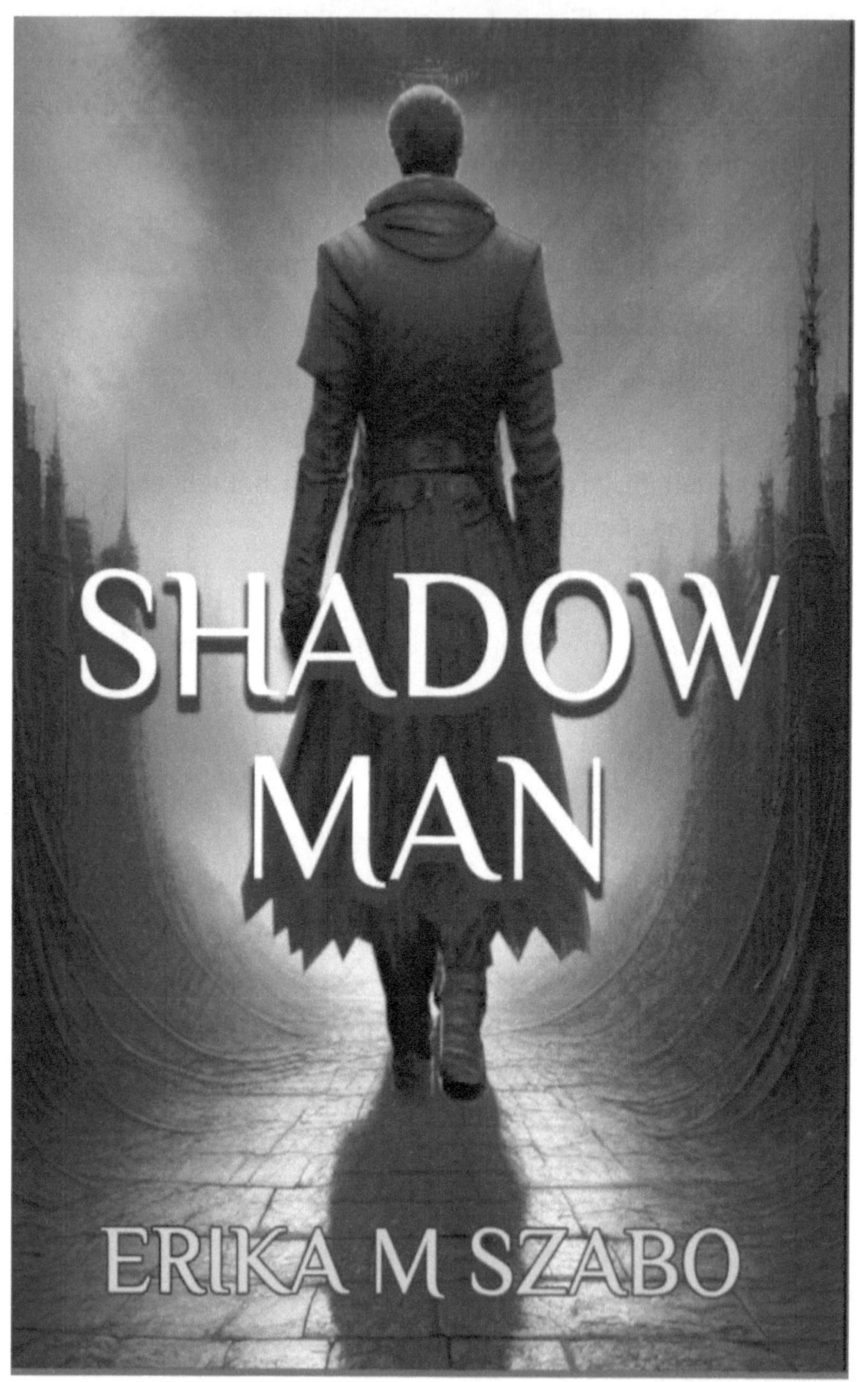
SHADOW
MAN
ERIKA M SZABO

The Watchers kept their eyes glued to the rapidly changing images on their screens as they monitored the predicted key events for the following day. A barely lit, air-conditioned room and ergonomic chairs provided a pleasant work environment, and eight-hour shifts with ten-minute breaks every hour were designed to protect them from exhaustion. However, their work was tedious.

So far, as for the effect of the following day's events, nothing has been flagged by the AI capable of monitoring five dimensions simultaneously and predicting a possible cause of major change in the future. The woman at the first station stretched and tried to relax her aching back. Suddenly, she froze when the "possible dangerous outcome" sign flashed on her screen. She tapped the sign to view the time and location. She read "August 4, dimension 5 in New York at 8:30 PM". She quickly tapped the communication button and reported to the commander, "Sir, dimension 5 has been flagged for tomorrow!"

The old man was startled by the urgency in the woman's voice and looked at her from his glass-enclosed office. "Send it to me!" he instructed and leaned back in his comfortable chair behind his desk. He looked at his screen and watched the rapidly moving projected scenes as a disheveled man attacked a young woman. He tapped the future prediction icon and after reviewing the possible outcome, he thought, *that boy must not be born from that sadistic attack!* The old man tapped the alternate future icon on the screen and viewed the woman's alternate future. Short scenes flashed on the screen in rapid succession. The woman embraced a man, they walked on the beach hand in hand. Next, the woman walking down the aisle in a white gown and a man waiting for her by the altar. The commander watched the hazy, obscured face of the man. "She doesn't know him yet." He murmured and continued watching the rapidly changing scenes. "Yes! Their son, with the guidance of loving his parents, will do remarkable things. Her attack tomorrow must be stopped."

The old man made his control unit screen visible on his forearm, and with a sweeping motion, he touched the communication icon. "Kirk," he said.

"Yes, sir," a pleasant voice replied almost immediately. "I'll be right there, sir."

The handsome, blond, athletic man in his mid-twenties recently joined the Enforcer Unit of six members. Each having their own apartment in the central building, Kirk was excited when after rigorous screening, he was chosen to join the team. This was for his special ability to jump the barrier seamlessly and safely between parallel dimensions. Only a few people were born with this ability, and others who tried paid a grave price for their attempts.

Kirk adjusted his black uniform and hurried through the long corridor toward the Watchers' room, feeling the pleasant tingle of anticipation. *I hope this goes smoother than the last job,* he thought as he entered and walked across the long room to reach the commander's office at the far end.

The commander in his late sixties raked through his white hair with his fingers, watching Kirk as he closed the door. He sighed. "Don't make a mess of this like you did last time!" He warned him with a stern expression while transferring the recorded future event to the young man's control unit but leaving out the prediction of the alternate future.

"It wasn't my…" Kirk started to speak, but the commander cut him off.

"You let them see you!" the old man accused. "And the 'Shadowman' video is still circulating on the 5th dimension net and fueling more conspiracy theories. It cannot happen again. Do you understand?" He warned the young agent.

"No, sir, I mean, yes, sir," Kirk stuttered, his cheeks turning red. "I had my control unit fixed, and it will never happen again, sir."

The old man nodded. "That man must be transferred to the 9th dimension. Here is the disk. Enter his data and inform the colony director of his arrival tomorrow." The commander handed Kirk a dime-sized, thin metallic disc.

"Yes, sir. I'll work on it, sir."

Right," the commander grunted and with a flip of his wrist dismissed the anxious young man.

Kirk hurried toward the door feeling the curious glances of the Watchers on his back and heard their muffled sounds of questioning each other.

"What did he do?" a woman asked in a soft voice. "The boss seemed angry."

And then a disapproving voice whispered, "Didn't you hear? He was seen, and the worst of it, the video will stay on their net forever!"

"Oh! So, he's the one they call 'Shadowman' then? How embarrassing!"

Kirk ignored the whispers and closed the door behind him. "It's so easy to judge!" he muttered. "They don't even think of blaming the technician who forgot to do the scheduled maintenance on my control unit and caused my cloaking device and speed control to malfunction," he fumed, hurrying through the deserted corridors to his living quarters. "Sitting at their station in their comfy chairs, they don't know what it's like to prevent future disasters in the real world. Moreover, not even in our world, but in a different dimension."

Kirk sat down, transferred the prediction file to his large screen, and watched as the young woman hurried down the deserted sidewalk. *She's a nice-looking girl, and she has such a kind face.* he thought when his thoughts were interrupted by the bulky man's attack. Kirk's anger escalated when he saw the cruel, lustful expression on his face as he grabbed her with brutal force and kept dragging her to the dark alley. She fought her attacker with all her might, to no avail. Kirk wanted to scream and stop watching the prediction, but he knew he had to see every detail. He kept watching as the man subdued her and threw her on the ground. When she kept wiggling her body and furiously kicking, the man hit the side of her head with such force that it made her lose consciousness. He grunted, tore her clothes off, and viciously violated her limp body. Then he stood up, and as if nothing happened, he walked away leaving the unconscious woman lying on the ground, her legs apart, half naked.

Kirk jumped up and slammed the desk with his fist in frustration. "And it's not the first time! This bastard deserves to be locked away for good!"

Feeling a bit calmer, he sat back down and watched the rest of the future predictions. The young woman was spotted by a man who was walking his dog. He called the police and ambulance, and the woman was taken to the hospital. Physically she recovered within a few weeks, but the devastating psychological effect and finding out that she was pregnant, held her tightly in its grip. Her doctor mentioned that she had the choice of terminating the pregnancy, but she firmly refused. "The baby is innocent and deserves to live," she concluded.

Kirk watched the woman giving birth to a boy. Growing up, the boy would show signs of cruelty and lack of compassion early on. He'd have a brilliant mind and would become a scientist. In his mid-forties, he'd discover the parallel dimensions, and fueled by his hunger for power and control, he'd end the long period of peaceful existence between the multiple dimensions. After viewing the woman's predicted alternate future, Kirk set to work on the plan.

***

Feeling tired after her twelve-hour shift in the busy ER, Emily kicked her shoes off and massaged her achy feet while giving reports on her patients to Cathy, the night shift nurse. "You look exhausted!" Cathy said with the smile of an empath. "Did you pick up extra days again?"

"Yeah. Two of our nurses are sick, so we all had to pick up extra shifts," Emily sighed. "It's been a long five-day stretch but finally, I'm going to be off for three days."

"Enjoy the time off. You need to recharge," Cathy said, standing up and turning toward the patient rooms.

Emily stepped into her shoes and joined the dayshift nurses in the locker room. On her way to the bathroom, she peeled off her wrinkled uniform and threw it in the hamper. After scrubbing her hands and arms, she washed her face and walked back to her locker letting her long auburn hair out of the tight bun. "Ahh, that feels good," she mumbled with a deep sigh enjoying the relaxing feeling as her hair tickled her bare shoulders and upper back. Putting her jeans and t-shirt on, she grabbed her bag, waved goodnight to the chattering nurses, and headed to the garage.

As usual, the traffic crawled on the Parkway, but finally, Emily reached her exit and turned toward her quiet, residential neighborhood. She drove around the block looking for a space to park her car. Feeling nervous, she finally spotted a tight space a block away from her building, barely enough to squeeze her Mini Cooper between a car and a pickup truck. Locking the doors, she started walking and quickened her steps as she hurried down the strangely deserted sidewalk.

She had never been one to scare easily, but there was something about this particular evening that made her skin crawl. Perhaps because she was tired, or it was the way the wind howled through the branches of the trees lined up by the sidewalk or the way the streetlights cast eerie shadows across the pavement.

Suddenly, footsteps echoed loudly in her ears, and she could feel the presence of someone behind her. She turned around quickly, but there was nobody there. *I must have imagined it.* she thought and quickened her pace trying to shake the feeling of unease that settled in the pit of her stomach. But the footsteps continued to follow her, growing louder, and sounding closer with each passing moment.

She was afraid to stop to look back, when suddenly, she felt a strong grip on her arm, pulling her toward a dark alley. Emily gasped, her body tensing as she tried to break free. But the hands were too strong, too firm, and she found herself being dragged backward into the shadows.

Emily tried to scream, but a hand clamped down over her mouth, muffling the sound. She grabbed his wrist and struggled against her attacker, but he was too strong. For a moment, Emily's mind went blank with terror. She knew what the man's intentions could be and it terrified her. Her heart felt like it was going to explode, and she could hardly breathe.

"Be quiet," the man's raspy, muffled voice growled.

Emily shook with fear as she felt the man's warm breath on her neck and the side of her face. She couldn't turn her head to look at her attacker. Kicking the man's legs, she kept twisting her body, but the strong man just grunted and kept dragging her. Her mind racing, Emily desperately tried to find a way to escape and felt the furious rage building inside her. *I'm not going to make it easy!* She shouted in her mind and held the man's wrist tighter while slowly lifting her other arm to gain leverage.

"Easy now, pretty one!" the man whispered. "You'll enjoy it, you'll see." He cackled with sick lust in his voice.

Emily's rage peaking, she gathered all her strength and elbowed the man's ribs as hard as she could. She heard the sickening sound of bone cracking as the man threw her to the ground and yelled out in pain. "You little bitch! I'll kill you!"

Expecting the worst, Emily watched with horror as the man's body was jerked backward by an invisible force and flew across the alley hitting the stone wall with a loud thud. Sitting on the ground she stared at the crumpled, still body of the tall man in disbelief. Suddenly, she felt a sudden, cold wind, and the loose dirt stirred up by the gust of wind hit her face. Trying to protect her eyes, she quickly covered them with her hands. The wind stopped as abruptly as it started, and she peeked between her fingers. Her attacker was gone.

She turned her head to look around and was startled when she saw a fleeting dark shadow from the corner of her eye. "Who's there?" she shouted as she struggled to get up while frantically looking around.

Someone threw him at the wall as if he was a ragdoll. But he's not there. What happened? She couldn't find any explanation. Emily shivered and on shaky legs started running toward the street.

She found her bag on the sidewalk and ran toward her building. Out of breath, with trembling fingers, she fished the keys out of her coat pocket and opened the door. She rushed inside, slammed the heavy door behind her, and ran up the stairs to her second-floor apartment. Safely inside, she slid down to the floor, sobbing.

***

Kirk grabbed the unconscious man and pressed the small disc, that was given to him by the director, to the man's forehead. He watched as the metallic disc heated up and burned itself to the man's flesh. Satisfied, he tapped the maximum speed icon on his control pad, which was built into his forearm, and stepped onto the platform of his nuclear energy-powered traveling device, dragging the man with him. *She's safe now,* Kirk thought glancing back at the woman before they jumped through the barrier of the 9th dimension and continued the high-speed flight toward the mountains. Feeling the pressure in his entire body made him nauseous, but it was over within a minute.

Regaining his balance, he dropped the man at the gate of the heavily fenced colony and reported to the guards. The guard touched his scanning device to the disc on the man's forehead and nodded. "We have a long list on this piece of garbage, he hurt a lot of people in his miserable life," he said, looking at the man at his feet while two guards shackled the man who was beginning to regain consciousness and started trashing and screaming.

"He's strong as an ox," Kirk exclaimed as he watched the guards dragging the man on the ground, and they threw him into the armed vehicle.

"Yes," the guard cackled. "The director assigned him to work in the coal mines. Until his last breath. But why wasn't he brought in sooner?"

Kirk scratched his ear and sighed before answering, "Somehow, he slipped through the cracks of the 5th dimension's police. He wasn't even the suspect of the multiple crimes he committed. And you do know that we can't interfere until the effect of the criminals threatens our peaceful future, but finally, he was flagged by the prediction AI."

"I know," the guard sighed. "Our world is still not even close to perfect until people like him will not be allowed to be born."

"I wouldn't mind not needing our jobs in a perfect world."

"Neither do I," the guard chuckled. "See ya next time." He said goodbye as Kirk stepped onto his traveling device and sped off.

***

Emily knew someone saved her from the brutal attack, but going through every second of the evening didn't help to find who it was. She saw only a shadowy figure holding the man who attacked her, and they disappeared in a flash. *Could that be the "Shadowman" people are talking about on the net?* she thought. But the kindness and warmth she sensed when the invisible man saved her, stayed with her.

Despite the plethora of theories swirling around in her mind, Emily couldn't shake off the feeling of unease. No amount of online research or well-meaning advice from strangers could dispel the sense of foreboding that gripped her heart. She kept searching, hoping for some rational explanation that would put her fears to rest that had been haunting her for weeks.

***

Kirk's thoughts were occupied by Emily, and he often made unauthorized jumps through the barrier of her dimension to watch her daily life. He was infatuated with her more and more with every jump and fantasized about the possibility of turning off his cloaking device and introducing himself to her. As Kirk watched Emily from the confines of his cloaking device, he felt a deep sense of longing growing within him. Her resilience in the face of danger, her determination to find her mysterious savior - it all drew him closer until he could no longer resist the pull of fate.

One fateful evening, as Emily walked home from work, the streets deserted and a storm brewing overhead, Kirk made a decision that would change both their lives forever. With a deep breath, he disabled his cloaking device and stepped out from behind the tree, his eyes fixed on Emily.

Startled by his sudden appearance, Emily stumbled back in shock, her heart racing with a mixture of fear and curiosity. But as she looked into Kirk's eyes, she sensed something familiar - a kindness and warmth that seemed to echo the presence of her mysterious savior.

Without saying a word, Kirk extended his hand toward Emily, a silent invitation for her to trust him.

"You... you're the one who saved me," Emily whispered, her voice barely above a whisper.

Kirk nodded solemnly, his heart pounding in his chest. He decided to tell her everything.

***

One of the Watchers drew a sharp breath, quickly tapped the communication button, and reported to the commander, "Sir, something is happening in dimension 5… but I don't understand. Kirk and..."

The old man startled by the confusion in the woman's voice and the mention of Kirk, looked at her from his glass-enclosed office. "Don't let anyone else see it!" he barked. "Copy the file to a disk, bring it to me, and then classify the file," he instructed.

"Yes, Sir!" the woman said, her fingers rapidly moving on the keyboard. She took the small disk, walked to the commander's office, and handed it to the old man.

"Not a word about this to anyone!" the commander said.

"Yes, Sir," the woman replied, nodded, and hurriedly left the office.

The commander's eyes were fixed on the projection of the AI-generated future, his brow furrowed in concentration. As the image sharpened, the man's face became focused, and he let out a small sigh of relief. "Ah, just as I hoped, it's you, Kirk," he said, a smile spreading across his face. "Your son will be the one to save us. Another successful prevention for the betterment of mankind." He leaned back in his chair, a look of great satisfaction on his face. The delicate hum of his projector filled the room as the prediction continued to play out before him, depicting a world free from destruction and chaos. It was a moment of triumph, and the commander couldn't help but feel a swell of pride for their mission and its ultimate goal - a brighter future for all humanity.

CAREFUL WHAT YOU WISH FOR
DAVID W. THOMPSON

All Hallow's Eve has been my favorite holiday for as long as I can remember. Maybe it began with a juvenile sweet tooth. Still, way before I traded in my fireman and clown costumes for Count Dracula, the Mummy, or other infamous purveyors of darkness, Halloween stirred my dark heart. And why wouldn't it? Everyone, well, almost everyone, enjoys a night of revelry and the opportunity to be someone else for a few hours. I wished Halloween had come around every weekend.

As I matured, I dreamed of finding a wife with similar interests— a "nice" Wiccan lady, maybe? The Goth craze was heaven-sent for me—perhaps not heaven, but you get the idea.

My mother often warned me, "Be careful what you wish for, Victor." But I was born in the land of Moll Dyer, the Winter Witch. As a scion of one of the families suspected of her demise, my proclivities were ingrained into my psyche for generations. So, it wasn't my fault; I had no choice.

It seemed predestined that I would meet Brianna at my friend Tony's Halloween party. She had long black hair, emerald green eyes, a pale complexion boasting scattered freckles, and a dimple on one cheek. She was dressed as a witch (of course), but not the store-bought "sexy witch" nor the wart-nosed, green-skinned hag. Her dress was a turn-of-the-century antique draped with a grey hooded cloak. She wore a triskele necklace with spiral earrings to complete her look. Her smile lit up the room, but I sensed a secret darkness. Yup, it was love at first sight.

Our courtship began immediately. By Thanksgiving, she confided that she was an Old Order witch…not a modern-day Wiccan, she assured me, but a genuine witchy witch. I wasn't quite sure what that meant. I asked her if she was a white witch or a black witch.

"Which witch would you prefer?" she asked with a mischievous smile.

"Can't I have both?"

Bri raised one eyebrow in response, her lips drew into a taut straight line, and her eyes narrowed.

"Be careful what you wish for, Victor."

"You know you've captured my heart, Brianna. Even my kitty, Daisy, has fallen under your spell." Daisy lifted her head from Bri's lap at the sound of her name.

"Then take heed of my warning, my love. It isn't too late for you to walk away, and I'd not hold it against you if you do. But if you're in, make sure you're all in. Loyalty to me and respect for who I am…these things I require. It won't bode well for you otherwise."

I only smiled at her thinly veiled threat, though she didn't smile back. It wasn't as if I had a choice in the matter. She was always in my thoughts, even in my dreams…especially in my dreams. Ah, the things we did in my dreams… Even now, I blush at the thought, and my blood stirs at the memory. But any physical love was only in my dreams. Brianna swore a pact to her coven to remain chaste until marriage. I could wait.

Her spell on me was absolute, and we set the wedding date for Halloween; what could be better?

***

Our bachelor and bachelorette parties were planned for the Saturday night before the wedding. I was to leave at 8 o'clock to meet my friends at Anthony's house. Brianna was picked up an hour earlier when a bus pulled up in front of my apartment. Ghouls, vamps, demons, mummies, and even one wendigo were in attendance and hanging out the bus windows. Brianna was dressed in her outfit from our first Halloween together—my witch.

The neighbors with apartments facing the street were also staring out of their windows. I assumed they were as jealous of the partygoers as I was until I heard old Misses Janis yell, "John, come quick. There's a whole busload of freaks outside."

The riders "Booed" at her and made off-color hand gestures. Brianna pretended not to notice any of it.

"Who are all of those people?" I asked.

"They are my family, Victor, my coven."

"Are they the same ones you meet every full moon when you wear your outfit? The nights when I'm not invited?"

"It is more than an "outfit." It's who I am, Victor. And you'll be invited soon enough, my love. After all, Halloween falls on a full moon this year, and it's a blue moon at that."

"But it's our wedding day…"

"And, of course, they'll be there, silly," she winked and ran off towards the bus.

There was a rowdy cheer when the revelers saw her step from my doorway. I knew my night would be filled with drunken bravado and ladies of ill repute strutting their assets for my friends and me. Once, I would consider that a night of supreme entertainment. But Brianna's night? I knew her party would surpass anything, my dear, but vanilla friends might conjure up. As the bus pulled away from the curb, I wished…never mind.

The bachelor party went as expected. There was too much alcohol, minimum inhibitions, and maximum female exposure. I felt guilty about the last part. I didn't act inappropriately but could only think of two things. One was Brianna telling me I was her first boyfriend and she'd never been with a man. The other thing was her admonition about loyalty…

After too many bourbons, Tony became awkward, unresponsive, and aloof.

"What's going on with you, Tony?" I asked.

"Victor, I don't know how to tell you this. You're my best friend, and I love ya, man. Besides, I will be your best man next week."

"Spit it out, Tony. What's the deal?"

"You're right. That's probably best. So here goes… I've been dreaming about your fiancé, Victor. Nothing happens in the dream…not really, but she is your betrothed. You're like a brother to me, my brother."

"That is a bit strange," I answered, "and creepy, to be honest. I wish you'd kept that tidbit to yourself. Still, it was a dream, Tony, and dreams aren't real. Let's please forget we had this conversation and have another drink."

***

The long-awaited day of our nuptials finally arrived. The nondenominational church was packed with friends and family. I'd never met any of Brianna's family. She'd said her coven was her family, and they were…literally. The same folks at her bachelorette party sat in the front row. Her family was dressed the same as then, though most left their masks at home… The Wendigo man waited in the back of the church to walk her up the aisle.

On the groom's side, my family fidgeted and whispered to each other behind their hands. When one of the men from the "other side" (one of the vampires) brushed against my mother's arm, she recoiled as if shocked, rolled her eyes, and turned as white as the north end of a southbound rabbit. I tried not to smile and bit my lip until I tasted blood.

My bride entered five minutes after the appointed hour, and all eyes were on her. She was a vision, and my dream was made real. The Wendigo man marched her up the aisle, keeping in time with the wedding march, and my heart was full.

We had decided to write our vows. I don't remember much of mine. I promised to love her forever, be loyal, and respect who she was—the usual heartfelt but trite redundancies. I remember Brianna's, though, word for word.

"I promise to love you forever from this day forward. I will walk in your dreams until the end of your days. Your pain shall be my pain;

even that which I inflict, we shall share. The One who presides over us all shall bless our union. Our children will inherit the Earth. The world above and below shall bow to our progeny, such devotion our love shall have wrought. Until another's dream is born, we shall be together. To break our vows means death, but even in death, you will be mine."

***

The reception followed at the American Legion Hall on Sixth Street. It wasn't a high-brow joint by any stretch of the imagination, but it suited us and our budget well. The food was excellent. We didn't skimp on the caterer, and the open bar kept the adult beverages flowing.

Tony gave a heartwarming speech about our long friendship and our non-blood brotherhood. I feared bourbon was taking its toll on him again when he mentioned Brianna's beauty and how she'd be any man's dream. I shot him my best rendition of an evil eye, and he winked concluding his speech to much applause. He passed the microphone to the Wendigo man.

"I haven't known Victor for very long, but from what Brianna has told us and from the private investigator we hired, he is a perfect match..."

The room laughed, although no smile creased Wendigo Man's face.

"Where was I? Ah, yes, Victor seems the perfect match for our princess. I think he will fulfill her and her family's dreams. At first, I was concerned about their age difference." *What?*

He continued. "Brianna has searched long for a heart that would beat in unison with hers, with a matching appetite and a shared dream they can bring to fruition together. In Victor, we've found our man. Please raise your glasses to this loving couple in the presence of our Lord and us, the family and friends who love them."

I tossed back my champagne or a reasonable facsimile...it was bubbly, at least. I knew I'd imbibed too much when I placed the glass

100

back on the table. From the corner of my eye, I spotted the shadow of a horned beast man streaking across the back of the dance area.

I pushed my chair back, wide-eyed. "What was that?"

Brianna took my hand. "It was nothing, my love. Perhaps stick with wine and leave the bourbon for those who don't have marital responsibilities tonight?" She smiled her devilish grin.

I glanced around the hall, but no one else stared in horror at the back of the room.

The remainder of the reception went without a hitch. The cake was cut. Brianna didn't smash it into my face. We had our dance together. Wendigo man cut in, as did my mother. Tony caught the garter, and one of Brianna's "sisters" caught the bouquet. Seeing someone who was a demon a few nights ago sniffing the mass of daffodils cradled against her chest was weird.

Soon after, Brianna suggested we make our way home. Our honeymoon cruise didn't start until the next day.

"We have a busy night ahead, lover," she said. Each of her family members reiterated this sentiment as we said our goodbyes.

I happily agreed, as my mind was still in a fog and my gait unsteady. I prayed my performance that night would be up to par…no, superhuman. My beautiful bride deserved nothing less.

***

My vision became a kaleidoscope as we approached my apartment.

"Don't worry, Victor. I'll get you safely to bed…to our marital bed, my love. Trust me, and everything will come to pass… just as prophesized."

I laughed. "I love you dearly, Bri, but I don't think there are any divinations about our affections."

"It's all written, my love, but you needn't be afraid."

"I'm not afraid, Bri. I want everything to be perfect for you."

101

"And so, it shall be."

Brianna had to unlock my apartment door as I leaned against the door jamb. She helped me inside, where I flopped into my overstuffed recliner.

"I'll be right back," she said. It might have been minutes or hours before she returned. I was in no condition to judge time.

"Drink this," she said, handing me a glass filled with greenish liquid. "It will help sober you up and prepare you for what's ahead."

***

I woke up in my chair with a stinging pain in my chest. It was dark, a darkness so complete that I couldn't discern the accouterments in the room I'd spent so many hours in over the past five years. Chilled, I discovered my nudity. Brianna must have undressed me. Nothing left to her imagination now, I thought.

I touched my chest, and my fingers came away wet, but the strange sounds echoing from my bedroom…from OUR bedroom down the hall called for my immediate attention.

Voices…male and female chanting! I stood trembling at my bedroom door. I must be imagining it…did someone slip me something at the reception? *Brianna. Where's Brianna?*

"Diabolus…Diavolo…Diablo… Teufel…Master…

"The veil is thin; let him in.

"Light Bringer…Satan…Dominus…Lord…

"The veil is thin; let him in."

I threw open the door with Brianna's name on my lips. Around my bed stood a half dozen naked men and women. Two women approached me, took my hands, and pulled me towards the bed. The men stepped aside so that I might see what rested there. Brianna, my love, my bride, stretched across the bed, naked but for her triskele necklace.

"Deus noster benedixit. Our god blesses you."

"The veil is thin; let him in."

My head swam, and the shadowed image of a horned head raced across my bedroom wall. I pulled away, but the frail-looking women were strong…or I was too weak. They pulled me forward into my lover's embrace.

"The veil is thin; let him in."

"The veil is thin; let him in."

"It is written, my love," Brianna said. "The veil is this; let him in."

***

That night was the drunkest I'd ever been in my life. How could it not be when my recollection of the first time making love to the woman of my dreams was so distorted? For days, I still made excuses to Brianna that someone had slipped me a Mickey. I'd never experienced anything like it before.

She was understanding and pretended to agree, but I doubted her sincerity.

"It was all a dream, Victor…just a dream, and dreams aren't real. They can't hurt you."

"But I wanted it to be perfect…"

"As for me, it was an enchanting, blissful night. I regret that you cannot remember it… or what really happened anyway. It was beautiful, Victor, and I love you so."

"If I had any doubt before, I wouldn't now. You've taken care of me since I've been lying in bed. It can't be just a hangover, Bri. Maybe I should see a doctor."

"I'll always take care of you, Victor. Our dream has only just begun. But the doctor can't do anything we can't do for you here at home. He said as much when he came out for a house call two days ago. Don't you remember?"

"No, I don't. I must be losing my mind. Thank you, Bri. You never even complained about postponing our honeymoon, but I'll make it up to you. I'll never forget that or the Wendigo man's help. I don't know what herbs he mixes up, but I feel better after drinking his potions. The poultice on my chest helps me breathe easier, too."

"The Wendigo man? Oh, you mean Uncle Xavier?"

"Yes, but he'll always be the Wendigo man to me."

***

After two weeks, I was still too weak to move around the apartment alone. The virus still had a hold on me. Brianna or the Wendigo man helped me get anywhere I needed, even to the bathroom, although that was a significant improvement over the bedpan.

My bride was so upset by my forgetfulness of our wedding night that I began to pretend to have the memories. It wasn't hard with the information she'd shared with me. She was very animated whenever the subject came up. I was good enough at faking the memories that I started to believe in them myself. It was far better than my actual alcohol-induced memories of that night, and I usurped her memories as my own. When I came to terms with what really happened, just as Bri described it, my health also improved.

One morning, Brianna kissed me on the cheek before leaving for the grocery store. Wendigo man had left for home the day before, and I was alone to fend for myself. I wanted to make Brianna proud of me, something I doubted I'd managed thus far in our marriage. My strength was returning. It was time to get on with our lives.

When I felt a cramp, I pulled myself to my feet and shuffled towards the bathroom. Heck, I might shave while I was at it…

After the paperwork was done, I put a new blade in my razor and scraped away the two weeks' growth on my face.

The poultice on my chest curled at the edges, and I pulled it away. A mulch-like concoction of wet herbs dropped into the sink, making a mess I couldn't leave behind for Brianna to see. I cleaned it up and then wiped the slop off my chest. Looking in the mirror, a pale pink scar stared back at me—an upside-down pentagram carved into my chest.

***

When Brianna returned from shopping, I was sitting in my recliner waiting, finally awake. I was angry, crestfallen, and felt bitterly betrayed.

"We have to talk," I said.

She closed the door behind her and placed the grocery bags on the floor. When she turned back to face me, she knew I knew. I expected apologies or even defiance, but she smiled her disarming smile.

"It's about time," she said. "I was starting to believe I'd chosen poorly."

"What happened that night? Was it just as I remember? Do not lie to me anymore, Brianna."

"What else have you forgotten, Victor? You are the dreamer. I am but the dream. Remember that and believe whatever you're strong enough to handle. Dream whatever reality you like."

"That's nothing but gibberish, Brianna. And just what is your reality?"

"I believe I'm pregnant, Victor. I haven't seen a doctor, but I know. I can feel it."

"Pregnant? Where do you see us going from here? I wish I'd never met you, Brianna."

I slept on the couch that night, a fitful sleep at best. Brianna came to me in my dreams as she has every night since for these long, lonely twenty-odd years. We made love in my dream, but not cuddly, gentle, romantic make-up sex. It was wild, passionate, and angry fornication. In the morning, I woke up exhausted, and she was gone. Nothing was left behind to indicate she'd been a part of my life, save a short-handwritten note:

105

"You wished me gone, and you are the dreamer, so it will be. You forgot your vows. I'll never forget mine. I will walk in your dreams until the end of your days. Your pain is my pain; even that which you feel I've inflicted, we share. Even now, another dreamer dreams, but for you, there will never be another. I demanded loyalty. My coven will enforce it. For what we shared, beware my once love. I'll see you in your dreams, Brianna."

I threw the note in the trash. My anger was fresh but softened by a deep sense of loss that I could not dispel. I sat in my chair and cried most of the day. I tried to convince myself it was all for the best, but the angel (or devil) on my shoulder asked what she had done that was unforgivable. It was part of who she was…the Brianna I fell in love with. When had I ever been as happy as when she walked by my side, together as one?

I always felt hell was not so much fire and brimstone as it was the denial of love. I saw it as being in a large, locked room with all the amenities one could ask for. But everyone I'd ever loved and all who ever loved me was on the other side of that door, a door I could never open. God, with her perfect love, waited there too. I found my hell then, but more was to come.

I knew I had to find Brianna to make things right and return to what we once had. After two days of moping, I called Tony and shared my sad tale with him over drinks at Bowman's bar.

"You really think those things happened on your wedding night? What if someone drugged your drink? Could you have imagined the whole thing? You gotta admit it sounds bizarre."

"Brianna had me convinced of that for a while." I unbuttoned my shirt to expose the small pink pentagram scar on my chest. "But does this look imaginary to you?"

"No, I must admit—that looks plenty real. By the way, do you know the dark-haired girl with the pixie haircut at the end of the bar?

She's throwing some flirtatious looks your way. I won't judge. You know what they say about falling off a horse…"

"Yes, I know her, don't you remember? She was the "demon girl" who caught the bouquet at our wedding. She's a member of Brianna's coven. I guess it's already started just as Brianna said it would."

"You need to come home with me and talk to Naomi. You know she's into all that Wiccan and paranormal stuff. She'd have better advice than I can give you."

***

We left the bar after finishing our bourbons. Tony lived two blocks from the bar, in the opposite direction from my apartment building. At every turn and by every storefront, eyes stared back at us, lingering just a bit too long. Were they all part of Brianna's coven?

Naomi's eyebrows shot up when she saw me walk through her door.

"I didn't expect to see you so soon, Mr. Newlywed. Surely the blush isn't off the rose already?" She asked.

Tony must have shot her a look. "Oh, no. Victor, I'm so sorry."

"It's OK. My mother always warned me to be careful what I wished for. When my father's store failed, he said maybe some dreams are best unrealized. I think I've had a Master class in both adages."

I told Naomi everything I'd shared with Tony, leaving out everything above a PG-13 rating. Her advice was sobering.

"What have you gotten yourself mixed up in, dear friend? Your wife is no Wiccan, Victor, and her band of merry men and women is no coven; they're a satanic cult. She wrote that the coven would enforce your loyalty. Didn't her vows say, 'To break our vows means death?' Or something similar?"

"Yes, that's it exactly. I thought it odd at the time."

107

"I'd say. Tony and I have been talking about her vows all week. You said they marked you? Can I see?"

I bared my chest, and Naomi shook her head.

"I'm no expert, but from what I've read, they can track you from that mark. If the wound ever festers or gives you an odd sensation, heed it as a warning and move from where you are. But if they become aggressive or violent, you must pull stakes—for your sake and anyone close to you."

I thanked Tony and Naomi for their advice and commiseration. Despite Naomi's warnings, I wasn't overly concerned about the cultists. The whole idea of a cult hunting me down was medieval. I couldn't wipe the smirk from my face for the entire walk home. Naomi had spent too much time living in the world of her fantasy novels. I must have harbored some misgivings, though. When I approached my apartment door, the scar on my chest burned. I hoped it wasn't getting infected.

The building manager had yet to change the bulb in the hallway, and I felt my way to the doorknob and slid in the key. The floors were nasty, too, and my sneakers stuck to the tiles. I threw open the door and heard an extra "thump" as it closed behind me. Flipping on the light switch, I saw her…Daisy.

A rope tied under her shoulders held her suspended to the door. A surgical incision ran from her chest down to her groin. I wrapped my innocent kitty in a pillowcase and put the remains in a wooden box. I took her downstairs and placed it in the dumpster. I couldn't risk staying until I could find an appropriate resting place. I asked for her forgiveness, thanked her for being a loving companion, and went upstairs to mourn another loss.

My apartment was no longer safe. I slept in a hotel that night, only once waking to a burning hellfire on my chest. The following day, I withdrew all my meager savings from the bank, terminated my lease, quit my job, and left my apartment forever. Brianna and her coven left me no choice.

***

Twenty Halloweens have passed since the events I began in this narrative. It's said that the only thing constant is change. That's been the case for me through those years. My current residence is a ramshackle apartment on Louse Alley, so-called by the locals. I don't know the official name, but I'd bet Louse Alley is the most descriptive. Drug dealers, gang members, and ladies of the night populate the streets when the sun goes down and attempt to be invisible in the light of day. This is the thirteenth place I've lived since Brianna, not counting the one-day to a-week stopovers in flea-bitten (or bed bug-bitten) no-tell motels.

I knew they were always watching, waiting…I could feel their eyes on me, but for what? Was prolonging my agony their goal? When strangers on the street stared for a moment too long, I still wondered if they were part of Brianna's "family." Were they there to finally end it all?

Eight years ago, I imagined they'd forgotten me. The pentagram hadn't flared with unholy fire for months, even though my search for Brianna never stopped, and the trail was cold. I was so confident about my future that I asked a lovely waitress from the corner diner for a date. I didn't share my life experiences with her, though we drew close in the following months.

Susan was the opposite of Brianna, a breath of fresh air. She was conservative in dress and speech, attended regular church services, and was humble in nature. I thought she might be the one, a new dream. I went so far as to window shop for a ring at the local pawn shops.

I planned to pop the question at our six-month anniversary picnic. We were to meet in the park at noon, but she was still a no-show at one o'clock. My luck, I thought. She must have sensed my intentions and ran like hell. Probably best…

I stayed in a broken-down house trailer back then and dragged myself home to lick my wounds. The rooftop antenna only picked up four channels, and the signal was so weak that all the shows were in black and white. That was for the best when the six o'clock news aired. I'm not sure I could've stomached the sight of my girlfriend's body parts scattered across the highway. They never found the driver of the hit-and-run vehicle. Witnesses said he was wearing a horned mask. The sheriff said eyewitness accounts weren't always accurate. But Brianna had kept her promise: "For you, there will never be another."

Last year, I picked up a newspaper that some homeless guy left on the street. The front-page article was about an eighteen-year-old wonder child. She'd just been accepted for a full ride at the local university majoring in political science. She said her ambition was to ensure equity in every walk of life. Her bio claimed she treasured loyalty above anything else in a friend. Her name was Victoria. She had her mother's smile.

My dreams have always been of Brianna, even after all these years and all the pain. She comes to me just as she was then, a mixture of innocence and deviltry painted on her face, the perfect aphrodisiac.

What was my life's dream is now my daily hell. The saddest part? I still ache for her touch and love her with all I am… I always will… even in death, I'm hers.

SHEBAT LEGION
Happily Ever
After, and After

I have enough tickets saved for an hour at The Memory Bank. I wished I had been more insistent that we record more events. But if there weren't as many memories to choose from, at least the ones I had were good. I sifted through them on my way to my battered little car, trying to decide which one to relive today.

"Nice day!"

I give a startled little nod to The Girl as she jogs past, face covered in a breathing mask. I never learned her name, although she did tell me once. I was embarrassed that I had forgotten it, so she became The Nice Girl Who Jogs. Her young body is almost ferocious in its health and spandex. I wave at her with some cheer. The Nice Girl Who Jogs is also The Nice Girl Who Helps Carry in Groceries, The Nice Girl Who Can Be Bothered To Talk To An Old Woman. If I had a daughter, she is who I would have chosen, but motherhood was something that didn't happen in my first marriage, and by the time you, my dearest, my true love, well, I was too old, and we had a cat instead.

I see Mrs. Hardwood panting down the sidewalk, and I hurry to my car; she is a talker and quite deaf, and how you would have chuckled at some of the excuses I have given to put a halt to the endless conversation she snares me with, but I allow it, she is as lonely as I am. What did I say the last time?

"I have to go. My pot is boiling, and I am shrinking heads today."

"Making bread?"

I snicker beneath my breath as I slide behind the wheel. Oh, I am not a good person, not as good as I should be. Maybe you wouldn't have laughed; perhaps you would have shaken your head in disappointment at my childishness. I guess we will never know.

I will visit Mrs. Hardwood later and present her with a bundt cake. This month's staple box included one of those quick and easy mixes. Being old and lonely isn't easy.

I drive carefully to The Bank. You would be proud to see me behind the wheel. I never drove while you were alive, and although you never admitted it, I could tell that you hated to be our sole chauffeur. You were the most cautious driver I have ever met, having every type of safety add-on and sensor, and you drove so slowly that Jogging Girl could have passed you easily. But now that I am on my own, well, public transport has too many people. You know how hard it is for me to deal with their chatter and confusing expressions. Small talk defeats me. But I can only walk so far, which isn't far at all; driving has become a necessity.

I made it to The Bank without incident and left the car in its assigned spot to charge. The lot is almost full, and a large queue will be inside.

Sometimes, being old has advantages, and I'm quick to move ahead in line when encouraged, maybe exaggerating my limp just a tad, inwardly cackling.

My turn comes, and I present my tickets to the passive-faced teenager at the kiosk.

"Please type in the date of memory or event; thank you."

She doesn't make eye contact as she slides over the check-in gizmo. There are few jobs for teens these days; she may consider herself lucky to have this one. She may not be smart enough to do anything else. But it is not her fault. We did this to our children with the atmosphere, modified foods, and unresearched pharmaceuticals. And, the truth is, most of the intelligent, ambitious ones left for Mars or the orbitals. At least it solved the housing shortage.

"3/25/24," I quickly type in, handing it back, taking note of her nails sporting a slowly spiraling nebula and not a few planets.

"Nice paint job," I offer kindly, and a wisp of a smile is aimed in my direction before she completes the next part of her task, letting me through the turnstile that points me down the hallway leading to the memory cubical.

I know the clinical coldness, as you put it, was one of the reasons you didn't want to record memories. It's true; a spartan factor is at play here, lots of white and chrome. It is any clinic, anywhere, but even so, it's a magical place. My step quickens, and my breath comes faster until my hand pushes on the door to the room with the throne and crown.

Okay, it's a chair and a cybernate head gadget, but magic by any other name is still magic.

I quickly slide onto the chair and wait for the technician, a nice fellow, who checks my name against the info on his pad and offers me a smile. I take a deep breath as the needle slips into my vein. There is a brief feeling of cooling in my extremities and nothing but stars as the program loads.

It is our trip to Niagra Falls. I remember it well, even without reliving it. Two old timers, touring around in floater chairs, our nights spent in a quaint hotel with an old-fashioned fireplace.

And. I am there. And you are there.

I feel the splash of the water as our boat passes through the falls, and I would like to swear that it is the water from the spray and not the tears on my cheeks, but I can't say for sure.

We are walking down the main concourse, wax museums, and other beckoning attractions on either side. The moon is rising over the falls, and it is perfect, and so are you.

We turn, startled, at the sound of squealing brakes.

Wait. No.

I pull you into the Museum of World Records. We marvel at the height of the tallest man and woman, wondering what that would be like. The world's, this one anyway, loudest burp is 107.3 decibels. You give a small burp, and I tell you that I believe the record is safe.

The next museum is one of the horror ones, and I hurry you through it, having no stomach for sights of people entombed, eaten by rats, or tortured. We exit quickly when a man dressed in black starts setting off crackers, *making me jump at the sound of the crashing car.*

No, no, wait.

The sound of the small firework leaves the smell of sulfur behind, *barely masking the sound of a car crashing into something somewhere.*

I have grown uneasy and don't know how that is even possible. This memory is a record; it is immersive, not interactive. I feel for the panic button beneath my finger and press it. The young tech comes rushing in, shows some relief that I'm not having a heart attack, and asks me what's wrong.

"I'm not sure," I answer truthfully. "There seems to be some sort of intrusion of events like someone else's program is trying to break into mine."

He looks bewildered, and I can't blame him.

"I apologize," he offers. "I will have our technicians look into the issue, and of course, we will refund your time." It was nice of him, especially since I was almost at the end of my memory. There wasn't much more: a nice dinner, a swim, a cuddle, too tired for lovemaking, and then sleep.

I miss sleeping with you, even the gurgle of your CPAC. You had a bum ticker, as you put it, and it was the reason we couldn't leave Earth for any length of time. You didn't talk about it much. I pushed you once, and you mentioned something about an accident and a broken heart, and you were so upset to say even that I never brought up the subject again. A trip to the space station at Luna had been enough to cure me of any desire I may have had to immigrate, I said. Nothing smelled right, and I always felt like I was falling.

Oh, I was such a liar. I loved being on that space station, but what was I to do, make you feel bad for stranding us on Earth when both of us wanted to leave it? No, pretending to a fear that didn't exist was far better, so I took the blame. Maybe you even believed me.

On the drive home, I didn't feel the usual mix of joy and sadness that I usually feel after a visit to The Bank. When I opened the door of my little house, Beezle the cat was there to greet me as always, but the house felt emptier than it usually did, even though it has always felt empty since you passed. You were a quiet man, but I always felt your presence. And I always knew when you weren't there. I suppose I was starting to get used to it. Still, today, that feeling was as strong as it was in the beginning, and before I knew it, I was hugging the cat and wailing.

The beeping and vibrating of my wrist phone alerted me, and I let it go to text.

"Mrs. B, we have not found anything analogous to the recording to make it seem to deviate from its original format. Please let us know if there is anything else to report. Thank you."

I put the cat down and searched for a tissue, the concerned feline trailing behind me. I reassured him with a tickle beneath his chin and blew my nose. Maybe I would get another kitten, give Beezle a brother, and name him after you. But then I thought of how much you would have hated that, and it was a maudlin thought, wasn't it?

Later, I baked the bundt cake and took it over to Mrs. Hardwood's house. As I raised my hand to push the door notice, I heard the sound of screeching brakes and whirled, almost dropping the cake tin, but there was nothing to see, and soon, the sound was gone, leaving nothing but the chirping of unconcerned birds behind.

I remember thinking that it was a good thing you hadn't died in an accident, that it wasn't me reliving a memory of your dying like that. That it was somehow better than my hearing a phantom car crash was beside the point. This was not me losing my mind because of what happened; it was losing my mind over something that *hadn't*. Mrs. Hardwood opened the door to find me laughing, wiping my eyes with one hand and balancing a cake with the other.

One thing about talking to someone hard of hearing is that you hear yourself speak, repeating your words, or even shouting, as the case may be. As I listened to my attempts at explaining the hearing of car crashes, I heard myself say, "And so you see, Mrs. Hardwood. It appears I must be suffering from auditory hallucinations."

Put that way, I was both alarmed and annoyed, but later that evening, I logged into the clinic, chose the diagnostic tab, took the offered search capsule, and waited for the results.

All test results were normal, so I had to ask to speak to a representative. While I waited, I rehearsed what I would say, even as the sounds of a car crash echoed from the kitchen.

The auto doctor dispensed two more capsules to take before I went to sleep. I got ready for bed with a feeling of trepidation, as it's one thing to have auto bugs creeping through veins and arteries and another to have them crawling around my brain. Still, it made sense they would look there, so I heaved a big sigh, made some tea, swallowed the capsules, and then turned in with the cat beneath my arm.

In my dream, I am standing with my friends at an intersection, waiting for the light to change. We are not paying attention to much of anything except for the video on my friend's phone. We move as if we are one entity as the signal for the light change sounds, not looking up from the phone and giggling. Suddenly, a large black truck comes into view, and we freeze. The truck veers sharply, tires screeching, and drives straight into a pole.

I wake up nodding; yes, that is the sound I've been hearing; the thing is, most of the dream events never happened. Yes, my friends and I watched movies on the phone, not paying attention to our surroundings; hell, we were kids and did stupid things all the time. But. There was no black truck, no accident. My memory can be as faulty as the next older person, but I didn't remember anything like that, even sitting for hours, stroking the cat, thinking furiously. No, it never happened.

I alternated snoozing and pacing, waiting on my auto doctor results, and when they came back normal, I raged at my console, "I'm telling you, no matter what your results say, there is something wrong with me!"

I was on hold for over an hour. It takes that long to get routed to a real doctor, and they are usually stationed at the platforms circling Alpha Centauri, the accent so thick, you can barely understand a word they say.

Yes, there are still some real doctors left on Earth, but they are mostly the ecological type, off reseeding the planet, closing off entire countries, and turning them into nature preserves. It will all be nice when it's done, but that won't be within *my* lifetime. For now, our little blue planet is a pretty lethal place, and you don't go anywhere without a skin suit, or you get skin cancer faster than you can say, "atmospheric disturbances."

After a frustrating conversation with the doctor on Facetime, I got new capsules to swallow over one week and then an appointment to discuss the results—or lack thereof.

A week is long when one hears the sound of a car crash stuck on repeat.

I decided to cash in my returned hour at The Memory Bank. It was excellent; our vacation at Disney. If anything could cheer me up, this memory would.

Oh, we were so young, and yet we weren't. And that is a classic example of relativity. As we rolled down the streets of Disney World, balloons tied to our go-carts, I considered us old then; I remember thinking we were. Looking back, all these years later, I can only marvel that I had that thought. It's funny, and yet, it's not.

"Brenda."

We are in line for The Pirates of The Caribbean when the voice intrudes.

"Brenda."

In the memory, I turn my head to see a woman standing there, a strained smile on her face.

"Who is that?" I ask you, and you look to where I am pointing, but when I look again, no one is there.

Later, as I lazily watch you lounge on a flamingo floatie at the pool, the voice intrudes again.

"Brenda, I need you to help me, and in turn, I can help you."

I almost hit the panic button, but she gestured to me frantically to stop, and for some reason, I did.

"Brenda," she beseeched, *"I need you to prevent an accident from happening. I deserve to live my life; only you can make that happen."*

"Do I know you?" Oh, my hallucination looked so familiar!

"You do, "she answered vaguely. "But listen, I need you to help me; you are the only one who can."

"How?" I ask. I can't help it; I'm curious.

"I need you to stop the truck from crashing."

My expression says all I need to say.

"Yes, it all very," she gestures vaguely, *"sciency."*

Her expression looked sheepish, and I'm sure mine was a treat because that is when we began to laugh, and I knew we would be friends, whether she was a hallucination or not.

I stopped chortling long enough to ask, " now that you have my attention, can we turn the car crash sound effects off?"

I watched as she pushed invisible buttons as if sitting in front of a console.

"Yes, I can," she said, "that should do it."

"Okay, so make it quick. What's the deal? You want me to help, you said. How? Why?"

"I can't explain that either," she began. "As to what I need you to do, you need to go into your late husband's memory of the day of the accident, the day the truck crashed, and I need you to turn the radio channel from Country101 to StimHits with Doug and Sue."

"I can't do that," I replied, aghast, then added, "what crash?"

She looked at me sadly.

"The accident? My husband's accident?" I whispered. "*That* crash?"

She nodded.

"Look," I said. "I don't have access to his memory bank; even if I did, how do I change something in a memory? Obviously, *you* can, or you wouldn't be doing it, but..." I trailed off, feeling uneasy and uncertain. Playing someone else's memories is about the snoopiest of snoopy things one can do, and the agreement I signed with The Memory Bank is pretty darned strict with its privacy rules. I have a bug in my brain because of it. And I opened the door and let it live there, ready to squeal to the feds if I decided to go back on my word.

"There are ways around that," she assured me. "Don't worry about that."

"Alright, plain talk it for me. I do this, and then what happens?"

"It's what doesn't happen," she said. "The accident doesn't happen, and I don't die. Not that day, anyway. Not that way."

"Okay, and I'm not trying to be mean, but if you live out your life, then what? I don't mean to sound selfish, but what's in it for me? You are asking me to take one hell of a risk."

She smiled." I get my life back, and *you* get longer with your husband because he never got hurt that day, no injuries to his chest at all. He will live out his lifetime with you. We all win; it's a win, win, win.

I mull for a bit. "Sounds too good to be true."

She shrugs. "Sometimes, that isn't a bad thing."

"I need to think about it," I say finally.

"There is no time for that. Listen, it's either now or never; you have spent so much time resisting my communication we have run out of wiggle room; it has to be now.

"Like, right now? Now, now?"

"Yes, this moment, seize it, or it's gone."

So, what would you do if you had the chance to get your beloved back? What would you do if you could change everything?

"Okay," I whispered. "Tell me exactly what to do."

It was surprisingly simple. I pushed the call button on my chair and asked for my husband's memory to be loaded, and they did it. I'm assuming some kind of magic trick on her side, but I will never know; she never told me.

And. I trusted her.

But, I guess I would have done just about anything to get you back, even make a deal with the devil, and honestly, she didn't seem like she was one.

In the truck, you are driving, and I am playing with the A.C. And, it's my hand I notice first, smooth, unlined, a younger hand.

And there you are, my darling. You even had most of your hair.

I reach out to touch your cheek and murmur, "change the channel, will you, sweetheart? Let's listen to Stimhits."

You make a face, but you change the station because of course, you do; you always tried to make me happy.

And that was that, really. The memory ended. There were no explosions of light and sound; there wasn't a single anything different that I could tell until I tried to get up from the chair and set off the alarm.

A tech came running. "There, there, dear. What's all this? Let me help you, hon."

Awfully nice of her. Honestly. I am so weary.

Kind hands help me into a floater chair, and I hang on to her arm, legs floating behind me until I am safely strapped in.

Floating?

My hand clutches the tech, and oh, it is such an old hand, thin, covered with wrinkles and age spots. And, as I begin to cry, I think how I should have known that when something seems too good to be true, it always is.

Isn't it?

"I hope you are happy," I howl. "I hope you are getting some kind of sick kick out of this!"

"Who are you talking to, Miss Brenda?" The tech's voice is calm and soothing. "Let's get your daughter to take you home and get you settled. Memories can set a person off, can't they? You just hang in there."

Daughter?

I hear the door open. It's Nice Jogging Girl who is smiling at me and calling me mom.

But I don't have a daughter.

Except we did have one.

I just wish I could remember.

I wish I could remember *any* of our years together on this timeline, but I don't, and it sure can get awkward. I wonder if the other timeline daughter knew that this would happen. I like to think she didn't. Or maybe she thought this was an even trade. I will never know. At least, I don't think I will. Thinking about all the what-ifs, hows, and maybes gives me a headache, so I just leave it be.

Life is different now, and that's okay.

I stare at the Earth from my tiny apartment. I live on the space station with my daughter, Stacy, and my kitten, Beezle Two, although I sometimes call him Betelgeuse. Beezle, The First passed long ago. I don't remember it, but when I brought up his name the other day, I was reminded me that he lived a long and happy life and that I was there for him at the end. Sort of like me now, except I still don't have you, except that I did.

Mrs. Hardwood lives next door. She had a cochlear implant. We are best friends. Together, we play cards at the seniors center, even though I hate cards, and I know, somewhere, you are laughing.

Sometimes, I wonder who *really* sent Stacy to me.

No, I don't go to the Memory Bank anymore; I just don't feel the need to. It seems we were very happy, you and I, and we lived a long life together, and honestly, isn't that all I need to know?

I Love You
FOREVER
MARTHA PEREZ

Chapter 1

I Love You Forever

Nicole Storm

Grandpa Buck had always been my rock, teaching me to believe in myself and see the world as conquerable. I longed to be that little girl again, sitting on his lap, soaking in his wisdom and stories. Life felt simpler back then.

He filled my world with love and lessons, showing me kindness even towards the unkind and instilling a love for life's simple pleasures like books, cooking, hiking, and stargazing in the snow.

I'm all grown-up now… and alone. I worked as a hairstylist in a place called Hair and Flare. I enjoyed my job. Talking to people took skill and patience, and I was good at making them look their best. It was satisfying.

When Grandpa Buck fell ill two years ago, I feared the worst, especially given his age. I sat by his hospital bed, holding his hand as he slipped away, leaving a void in my heart that nothing could fill. He was my everything, the only one who loved me unconditionally. My own mother didn't want me. She was a wild cat, as Grandpa used to say… and then one day she overdosed. That had been a hard time for Grandpa and me, but we were there for each other.

Grandpa Buck had left me a cabin in Big Bear. I loved living here. I cherished every moment in the cabin, a place filled with memories of the only person who ever showed me love.

Life can play jokes sometimes. I found out I had breast cancer a few weeks ago. The chemotherapy wasn't easy. I felt drained and sick, barely able to move around.

I bought a lovely brown wig and headed to dinner at the village. I was tired almost all the time. It was starting to snow, and I put my arms up in the air and swirled. My boots sank in the snow, making me lose my balance, and I fell hard, knocking myself out. Someone poked me on the side of my back. My eyes opened to a handsome man smiling, and then the embarrassment happened… I felt the cold air on my bald head.

"Are you all right?" the cute guy said.

"Yes, I'm fine."

"Wait… here… is this your wig?"

"Give me that!" I snatched it and placed it on my bald head.

"I think it's backwards." He smiled.

I was mortified. My face was beet red as he helped me up. I thanked him, put on my wig the right way, and slowly approached the restaurant. I ordered a glass of wine, hoping to dull the chaos and awkwardness.

Then, the handsome man walked in and kissed the waitress on the cheek. *Too bad he was taken.* He took a seat at my table. The man was full of surprises, and his baby blue eyes watched my every move.

"Hi, I didn't tell you my name. It's Noah Campbell."

"Nice name. My name is Nicole Storm." I shyly said.

He kept smiling, and he ordered a beer. We started to get acquainted, and finally, Noah walked me home. I couldn't believe he was spending time with someone like me. At the door, he hugged me and asked if I wanted to go for coffee in the morning. I said yes of course.

The next morning, we met at Starbucks, drank extra hot coffee and ate blueberry muffins, and talked.

"This is really nice, Noah. But why me?" I asked.

"Because you are lovely. Don't you believe in being in the right place at the right time?" he answered.

That night, before I went to bed, I wrote in my journal about what a great day I had. I wanted Noah to like me.

Months passed swiftly, like a gust of wind. My hair, though short, was slowly regaining its length, and I had returned to work after enduring the ravages of chemotherapy, which had taken a toll on my body, causing me to lose a lot of weight. Despite the lingering effects, I was feeling better each day.

Noah had been a constant presence in my life during this time. Despite his demanding schedule as a paramedic, he made time to visit me. Witnessing the pain and tragedies in his line of work had motivated him to pursue a career dedicated to saving lives. His dedication and compassion touched me deeply, and I found myself falling for him, though it stirred a sense of fear within me.

When he wasn't around, or he didn't call, I missed him, and my anxiety soared. But when I caught sight of him, my heart fluttered with anticipation, even though we hadn't even shared a kiss yet! I wondered if he only saw me as a friend. I have to be careful. After all, I was battling cancer and undergoing chemotherapy. Rushing into things wasn't an option. But still, I couldn't deny the allure of his tall, tanned body and piercing blue eyes.

Noah and I had our regular Friday night dinner. I wore a red dress and a wig because my hair was short and thin. I felt shy about my looks, but Noah didn't seem to mind. We went to Captain's Anchorage, a cozy and romantic restaurant. We had wine, talked, and held hands. With him by my side, I felt like the prettiest woman in the world, and it seemed like no other women mattered.

"Nicole, we're moving fast, but I love you. I don't want to waste any time. I'm going to Africa for two months. Can we spend tonight together and get married when I return? Will you marry me?"

"Yes!" I exclaimed, filled with joy.

We embraced and walked to my place. He spent the night, and we made sweet love. Everything was happening quickly, but with Noah leaving on Monday, I knew life was too short to hesitate.

The next morning, we went hiking at dawn. The chilly air made me feel alive. I was deeply in love with Noah, and he was the first man I made love with. It would be very tough to be without him for two months. But the thought of being married to him when he returned would inspire me to wait patiently. He moved into my cabin after our intimate time together. It was nice to have a man at my place. I've been alone far too long.

On the eve of Noah's departure, we cherished our time together. It would be a long two months apart, but it gave me time to work and plan for our wedding. In the meantime, I would start looking for the perfect wedding dress.

Noah knew how much I loved our cabin, and we dreamed of living here together… forever. With the fireplace casting a warm glow, we kissed passionately, feeling like teenagers in love. We danced to soft music, cheek to cheek, and enjoyed the tiramisu with a hint of sugary spice, with just enough coffee to keep us awake through the night.

At the break of dawn, at the airport, I sent Noah off with a pout and tears streaming down my face. He assured me he would call at night and that he would miss and love me forever. As he boarded the plane, I couldn't help but imagine our future together, with cute children waking us up in the morning and kissing us goodnight. I knew it was jumping the gun, but I had to think of good thoughts.

I went back to work to keep myself occupied. I opened the salon and was busy cutting hair in no time. Everyone in town knew about my relationship with Noah.

Although I was busy, I thought of him the whole day. Before he left, I told him that I'd get a puppy. It could help me miss him a little less.

During the weekend, I visited a breeder in the village named Ted, who welcomed me with a smile.

"Come in and see the full breed baby German Shepherds. I have five… take your pick!" he offered as he led me to where the pups were being held.

"I'll take the black and brown. You cute little rascal! Come!" I said as I spotted the puppy I wanted. He was only four months old and loved to play.

I took him home with me, where I had already set up his doggy bed and toys.

"I have to find a name for you… how about Maxwell?" I asked.

He wagged his tail and seemed to smile at me in agreement.

As we settled in, Maxwell kept licking my face while we watched a cowboy movie. Then he slept through the whole thing. It was so good to have company.

Just as I was getting sleepy, the phone rang. It was Noah.

"How are you, sweetheart? I miss you so much!" I blurted out upon hearing his voice.

"I know, sweetheart. I can't wait to come home to you. Did you get the puppy after all?"

"Indeed, I did. Maxwell is the cutest of the litter."

"Maxwell? I love it. I have to go, sweetheart. I just wanted to say hi. Call me tomorrow."

"Ok. You take care! Bye."

It was good to hear his voice, but it also made me feel his absence more. I snuggled closer to Maxwell and watched until I fell asleep.

"Well, Maxwell, it's just you and me," I said to my puppy as we headed to work the next morning. He loved sleeping, but being just a baby, he also enjoyed exploring the world around him.

As the days passed swiftly, I realized I needed to make time to plan our wedding. With no family of my own besides my dear Grandpa

Buck, who had passed away, I decided to contact my old friend, Debbie. Tomorrow, we can start by finding my dress, flowers, caterers, photographers, and a venue. Whispering Woods seemed perfect with its forty acres, and Lake Geneva boasted three lovely ponds.

In one of our conversations, Noah mentioned wanting me to meet his family. The thought filled me with anxiety. What if they didn't like me? Or worse, what if they thought I wasn't good enough? Debbie shushed me, reminding me to go with the flow and trust that everything would fall into place.

So, Debbie and I decided to have a girl's day out, complete with lunch, shopping, and pampering ourselves with clothes, shoes, and face creams. By the end of the day, we were both beaming with happiness, remembering my Grandpa Buck's wisdom that happy women make better humans.

Back at home, I took Max for a walk and gave him treats, still feeling anxious at the thought of meeting Noah's family. *I'd have to call Maria to help me out.* She was a neighbor who I sometimes hired for her housekeeping services.

As night fell, I read a good book with Max beside me until we both drifted off into a deep slumber.

The next morning, I was greeted by Max's enthusiastic licks on my face.

"Hey boy, calm down," I chuckled, knowing he wanted to go for a walk.

It was chilly outside, so I bundled him up in a sweater before heading out. I couldn't wait for Noah to see our puppy and feel the joy of having him around.

I had a doctor's appointment that day. My chemotherapy continued and though it still left me feeling tired, the thought of Noah and our upcoming marriage kept me energized. Maxwell was a big help too. Taking care of him kept me from focusing on my aches and pains.

Chapter 2

Meet the Parents

Finally, Noah's two months had passed. I picked Noah up from the airport, and as soon as we saw each other, we ran into each other's arms.

"I've missed you so much!" I whispered in his ear.

"Well, baby girl, I missed you more. Where's Maxwell?" he asked.

"He's at home. I've been training him not to potty in the house. Let's go home, have dinner, and take Maxwell for a walk. How was Africa?" I asked.

"It was sad seeing all those children sick and some without a mother and father," he replied.

Noah sees so much sadness in his work, but he's a giver. While making dinner, I prepared stir-fry with lots of veggies, and Noah played with Max. We enjoyed the fresh evening air and strawberry shortcake with coffee. Noah noticed the new living room set I bought.

"You bought a living room set. Wow, it's lovely, sweetheart. By the way, my parents will be coming for dinner on Saturday. They want to meet the woman that stole my heart," he announced.

Panic raced through my veins. I was nervous to meet them. Noah has an older sister, Eleanor, and his parents are in their late sixties. Noah assured me everything would be okay.

I really hoped so.

The next day, after walking Maxwell and making breakfast, I prepared a pot roast for Noah's parents. However, I started feeling dizzy and nauseous, and my stomach rebelled against the breakfast I had made. Maria, the housekeeper, helped me get dressed and brought me water, but I asked her not to tell Noah. I didn't want to worry him about something that would pass in hours.

At dinner, Noah's mother made hurtful comments about my cooking and expressed concerns about my ability to give them a grandchild since I had battled with cancer before. Noah defended me, but I ran to the bedroom in tears. Later that night, I kept vomiting and decided to see my doctor the next day. Noah was apologizing for his mother's behavior the whole time.

I went to the clinic alone, and after some tests, my doctor delivered the good news that I was pregnant. Two weeks passed, and I still hadn't told Noah about the baby. I decided to wait until our honeymoon.

With the wedding approaching, I hadn't seen Noah's family for weeks. Debbie, my bridesmaid, expressed concern about when I would tell Noah about the baby.

"I'll tell him soon. There's just so much going on. Let's have lunch. I'm famished," I replied, changing the subject.

After lunch, Debbie and I went shopping and got massages. It was Love Woman Day, a day I treated myself to once a month. As the wedding day approached, work picked up, and Noah and I were both busy. Maxwell kept me company most of the time. But we would be taking a two-week vacation, so it was worth the sacrifice.

Saturday arrived, the day of our wedding, set to begin in the afternoon. Noah was staying at a friend's house, and we planned to meet at Lake Geneva. I couldn't contain my excitement to marry the only man I had ever loved besides my Grandpa. Noah saw me for who I truly was, and my heart was filled with joy at the thought of our future together.

As I prepared for the big day, there was a knock at the door. It was Debbie, my dear friend, bearing gifts of orange juice for me and a small bottle of liquor for herself. I admired myself in the mirror, dressed in my gorgeous white lace, long flowered sleeve dress, with a pink floral wreath crown adorning my head. Debbie made sure I looked beautiful, just as she always did.

"Debbie, you need to ease up on the drinking. You'll need to walk down the aisle and find a guy of your own," I teased her. "Noah's friends are cute."

"Do you think I drink too much?" she asked, perhaps realizing the truth in my words.

"Yes!" I laughed.

Debbie embraced me. "I want you to be happy, Nicole," she said, wiping her eyes.

As we walked out the door to the awaiting black limo, I felt like a princess. Nothing would stand in the way of our happiness on this special day.

When we arrived, pink roses adorned the venue. Everything was simply breathtaking. As the music began, I walked down the aisle with a smile, my heart fluttering at the sight of Noah, looking incredibly handsome in his black tuxedo with a pink bow tie.

At the altar, Noah was waiting for me, and he whispered, "You look so lovely."

Unable to resist, we shared a kiss. All I could see were his blue eyes as we exchanged vows and heard the words, "You are now husband and wife." Nothing else mattered at that moment.

We hugged everyone, but I couldn't help feeling disappointed that Noah's mother didn't come closer. But that's ok. This was my day, and I refused to let anything dampen my joy.

Chapter 3

The Hawaii Honeymoon

We bid goodbye to everyone, and as Debbie hugged me tightly, I whispered in her ear to take care of my beauty shop and Maxwell. She nodded in understanding.

We headed straight to the airport for our two-week vacation in Hawaii. Exhausted, I fell asleep for the entire journey.

"Sleepyhead, it's time to go. We're here," Noah gently woke me up with a kiss.

We grabbed our luggage and made our way to paradise, surrounded by fresh air and blue skies. We stopped by the market before reaching the condo right next to the beach. I was awestruck by the beauty of it all.

We walked to the beach, soaking in the sun rays, and lounged there for a few hours. I teased Noah, telling him I had something to tell him when we got back to the condo.

"Ok, let's go back. You have me intrigued."

"It's not what you think, cute guy." I laughed while giving him a sexy wink.

Back at the condo, after a passionate moment together, I gathered the courage to share the news with Noah. "I'm two months pregnant," I whispered.

Overwhelmed with joy, Noah couldn't contain his excitement.

"Oh, my God!" Noah started jumping on the bed with excitement. "I'm so in love with you. I will love you forever!"

We spent the rest of the day bathing, watching the beautiful sunset, and having a late dinner.

He took care of my every need. I had chosen a wonderful man. He called his parents to tell them the good news. I had no idea what his mother said, but I didn't care. We both wanted to be parents, and this was a good start to our marriage.

The first week in Hawaii was heavenly, but by the second week, I started feeling weak. We decided to go back early, but while I was packing, the pain intensified, and I began to bleed. I knew exactly what was happening.

"Noah, please, we can't lose the baby," I pleaded as darkness slowly took over.

"Hang in there, sweetheart," he said, trying to comfort me.

When I came to, I could hear the machine beeping. I could smell the cleanness. I was in a hospital…

I wanted to stay in the darkness, where it felt peaceful and safe, away from the pain of reality. Waking up meant facing what had happened, and I didn't want to deal with it. I heard Noah's voice calling me back, telling me it would be okay.

Maybe my baby is not gone… so why do I feel this emptiness?

My eyes opened, and the first person I saw was Noah, peacefully asleep beside me. Gently, I squeezed his hand, and he stirred, offering a sad smile. Gathering my courage, I asked about the baby.

"Sorry, sweetheart, you had a miscarriage," he said softly.

My heart shattered, and tears flowed freely as we both grieved the loss. It felt like we could fill a river with our tears. In the days that followed, I recovered, and I was sent home empty-handed. It was really tough to face.

Debbie waited for me at the cabin, comforting me with homemade soup and bread. She let me cry for hours, understanding how much it hurt. Noah went back to work, and I tried to cope with the pain. It was the hardest thing I'd ever been through.

I stayed home for a week, thinking about what the doctor had said about the miscarriage being due to typical fetal development. We still wanted a family, so we decided to try again when the time was right, as the doctor advised.

Even though we were hurting, Noah and I kept going with our daily routines in silence. Despite all the challenges, I found strength in the memories of Grandpa Buck, who always taught me to keep going through tough times. With my best friend's support and Grandpa's lessons, I knew I could handle whatever came my way.

Chapter 4

Back to Reality

It was hard to get back into the same routine after losing a baby that was growing inside me, even though it was only two months along. I felt so alone, mourning the loss. Noah suggested we go hiking a few weeks later. The day was perfect, with clear blue skies and Maxwell bounding ahead of us on the trail. For a while, we felt almost normal again. After dinner and putting Maxwell to bed, we made love.

But the third month felt like an eternity, and the pain of the memory remained. Despite that, we were hopeful and eager to try again for a baby. At work, I tried to stay positive, whistling and humming, even when dealing with grumpy customers. Debbie noticed my upbeat attitude but also sensed my underlying worries.

Two weeks passed, and I decided to take a pregnancy test. When it came back positive, I was overjoyed. I couldn't wait to share the news with Noah. That evening, as he came home from work, I prepared an enchilada with black beans and plenty of sour cream for him. After his shower, I kissed him.

"Wow, you are in a great mood, sweetheart."

"That's because I have lovely news." I smiled.

"Okay, what did you buy this time and how much?" He teased.

"I did not buy anything… I am pregnant."

"What?" Noah lifted me and turned me around, making me dizzy with happiness. "That's the best news ever, sweetie." Then, he realized he had to be careful with me. "I will spoil you every day of your life and love you forever, Nicole." He embraced me and, true to his word, took good care of me. Every day was fantastic.

But just as I reached the three-month mark, I started bleeding. Panicked, I called the doctor and went to the hospital with Debbie by my side. Noah rushed to meet us there. The doctors confirmed that I had lost another baby. I was devastated, and my heart ached with grief.

I couldn't bear to face Noah, fearing he might leave me because I couldn't carry his child.

Noah was in shock, but he was there for me. All I could think of was what his Mother had said: *"Can she carry a baby after the internal damage caused by the chemotherapy?"*

I couldn't shake off the words of Noah's mother, questioning if I could carry a baby after the damage from chemotherapy. Despite reassurances from the doctor that many women do carry full-term after chemo, I couldn't shake off the feeling of unfairness and envy towards other women who could have children. It was a difficult time, and Noah was scared too, but I knew we had to face this challenge together.

Depression crept in like a snake, making me avoid contact with others, and the mood swings only intensified the deep sadness and loss I felt in my soul. Noah brought me lunch, but I had no appetite and no desire to socialize… all I wanted to do was sleep. Noah must have called Debbie, my best friend, because she burst into the bedroom like a force of nature and flung open all the window shades, despite the painful brightness.

"What are you doing, Debbie?" I shouted as I covered my eyes with the pillow.

"Get out of that bed, Nicole. Stop playing the victim and be strong. If you don't, you'll lose everything."

She was right. Debbie helped me shower and styled my hair.

I cried through the whole process. I took Maxwell for a walk and made dinner for Noah. He smiled and hugged me, happy to see me up and about. We watched TV until we fell asleep, hoping the next day would bring a fresh start, longing for normality in our lives.

We carried on that way for a while, helping each other heal. But every now and then, the depression would hit, and the sadness would overcome me.

Debbie invited me to lunch and shopping one day. I was more excited about buying new clothes.

"Hey, Debbie, how are you?"

"I'm getting married soon," she replied.

"With whom, and why didn't you tell me about your love life?" I asked, puzzled.

"Nicole, you were going through so much I didn't want to burden you. Drake Tompson, Noah's friend from work, asked me to marry him."

"Debbie, I'm so happy for you!"

"There's something else I haven't told you. I'm pregnant, so we need to plan quickly," she said.

I was genuinely thrilled for my best friend. She had waited a long time to find love, and now she would become a mother, something I had always wanted to be. Life isn't fair.

We went shopping and spent the rest of the day feeling calm and cheerful. But as soon as I was alone in the shower, I couldn't hold back the tears. I should have been overjoyed by Debbie's good news, but I couldn't shake the feeling of envy that she was pregnant... while I wasn't.

Chapter 5

My Best Friend's Wedding

Debbie looked stunning on her wedding day, with just a few clouds in the sky. I did her makeup, and despite a few flaws in her skin, she looked radiant. Her tummy was already showing, so I had to help her hide it with a sheer fabric. Meanwhile, I was feeling queasy myself. I decided to take a pregnancy test, and to my surprise, it came back positive. But this was Debbie's day, not mine, so I kept my exciting news to myself.

The chapel was filled with pink and white roses as Debbie walked down the aisle toward her new journey. Drake's eyes sparkled with love as he saw his bride-to-be, and everyone stood in awe. They were deeply in love, much like Noah and I, and we felt incredibly fortunate to have found such deep love.

After the ceremony, we all went to the park for pictures and then to the reception. Noah held my hand as we entered, and we enjoyed the music, the food, and the company. As the night began, Debbie danced with her new husband. Noah and I joined them, holding each other close. It felt like magic, and we didn't want the night to end. I felt happy about becoming a mom and hoped I could carry the baby to full term.

Debbie and Drake left for their honeymoon in Puerto Rico, and I had to be back at the salon on Monday. It was my business, and I'd be missing Debbie for two weeks. I wanted to tell Noah about the baby, but I was scared of another miscarriage. Deep down, I was desperate for this baby.

When Debbie returned, her lovely tanned tummy was showing, and she talked endlessly about her vacation. But soon after, I started to cramp, and my worst fears were realized.

It was happening again... why is this happening to me?

I went to the doctor, and once again, he confirmed that I had experienced another miscarriage.

Driving back home, I felt numb. I drove slowly… maybe too slow. I didn't care. I couldn't face Noah.

I parked in front of the cabin, standing at the front door. Noah was waiting with concern in his eyes. He asked why I hadn't told him about the baby, and I explained that I didn't want to get his hopes up. He held me close until my tears subsided and then put me to bed, exhausted.

The next morning, Debbie popped in to check on me.

"Hey, sweetie, how are you feeling?' she asked in a gentle voice.

"I feel better than I deserve," I answered.

"Sweetie, you will be okay. You just need time to heal."

It was easy for her to say, I was the one with the miscarriages. I know it wasn't her fault. At that moment, I hated the world.

I finally gathered the strength to shower. I didn't talk or eat, feeling numb. Not even Noah could make me eat. All I wanted was to sleep with my sorrowful heart.

Noah and I started talking to a psychiatrist, Dr. Taylor Jones. It wasn't my idea, but the doctor said it would help us and ease the strain on our marriage. My husband had plenty to say, if you ask me, and I couldn't help but roll my eyes.

* * *

Taylor Jones

I've read their files. The couple looked intense, maybe afraid to discover the truth about each other. I'm here to help them feel better and lessen their hurt. I feel sorry for them… they've been through a lot. They have to deal with the pain to keep going in their daily lives. I'll assist them in handling their pain so it would be bearable, even though it won't disappear completely.

Case number: 16794

Name: Noah Brad Campbell

Sex: Male

Age: 34

Height: 5 ft 8 inches

Weight: 160 lbs.

Ethnicity/Race: American

****

Name: Nicole Storm Campbell

Age: 32

Sex: Female

Height: 5 ft 4 inches

Weight: 125 lbs.

Ethnicity/Race: American

Occupation: Noah, a Paramedic. His wife Nicole owns a beauty salon.

Diagnosis: 4 Miscarriages, Depression.

"Please, have a seat, Mr. and Mrs. Campbell. Let's start with a simple question. Noah, how have you been feeling about the loss of your baby?"

"I feel awful. Nicole didn't tell me she was pregnant. Keeping secrets isn't the solution. I deserve to know instead of being left in the dark."

"I didn't want to get your hopes up. Dealing with four miscarriages has been really painful," I said as I wiped away my tears.

Dr. Jones interrupted, "Have you thought about surrogacy or adoption?"

"I want to try one more time to have a baby," Noah said, adding that they would explore other options if needed.

* * *

Nicole Storm

It made sense that they might see me as hopeless, or maybe I just felt that way about myself.

We visited Taylor Jones once a month, which helped our marriage. It was good to talk and not keep everything inside. When I felt sad, I remembered how Grandpa Buck used to take me camping to cheer me up.

Noah and I took Maxwell camping for the weekend, and the nights under the stars were the best part. Being in the wilderness helped us forget our problems. Writing in my journal helped me deal with the sadness of having multiple miscarriages.

Dear Diary,

Today is the start of a tough journey for me. I'm facing challenges that test my strength and make me wonder if I'm strong enough. My heart hurts so much, and I don't know how Noah and I will get through this together. Will I survive this dreadful sorrow?

Our journey began with love and adventure, but now I feel like I'm stranded on a mountain, surrounded by uncertainty. The nights feel long and scary, with only the moon to keep me company.

I've been through a lot, but I'm still trying to find peace. Noah and I are facing this together, even though we're not talking much right now. I hope the psychiatrist can help us figure things out.

I guess we'll just have to wait and see what happens next.

Chapter 6

A Huge Surprise

A few months later, I was surprised to find out I was pregnant again. Noah and I were excited but kept it a secret, not wanting to get our hopes up too soon. We didn't tell anyone just in case I didn't carry the baby full-term… again. I took it easy, working part-time, and planned a baby shower for Debbie, who had just discovered she was having twins. She was worried about raising two babies at once, but I saw it as a blessing. To manage the salon, I hired two new employees and only took a few house calls before resting at home. Noah decided not to go to Africa this year so he could stay with me.

We invited friends and family to the baby shower.

"Where is Drake?" I asked as Debbie waddled to the front door.

"He's at work and said this party is for women," she replied.

"Not true. Noah and some of his coworkers are coming to support the twins," I said, dropping the subject as friends began to arrive with gifts.

We set up the food in the backyard and played games. Noah was a lifesaver, helping me and kissing me every chance he got. It felt wonderful to keep the baby a secret between us. I knew that in one more month, I would start showing. I couldn't wait to wear maternity clothes.

Enough about me. Today was about Debbie. It was time to cut the cake and open the gifts. Debbie was all smiles as she opened her presents. I got her two cribs and a cute Jeep Wrangler two-seater stroller.

After everyone left, I suggested Debbie stay overnight. I sensed something was wrong in her marriage. I asked Noah to take Maxwell for a walk and then asked Debbie to sit down.

"What's going on with you and Drake?" I asked.

"He's having an affair, and he's leaving me, Nicole. When he found out about the twins, he wanted out. What will I do without a husband and the father of my children?"

"I'm so sorry, Debbie. You will be a wonderful mother, and you will be strong. I will help you as best I can," I whispered in her ear. "I'm pregnant too."

"Oh, my God, I am so happy for you, Nicole," she exclaimed, and we embraced.

We spent the night giggling, snacking on leftovers, and sorting the baby gifts. The baby clothes were adorable. We were best friends and would help each other through the good, the bad, and the ugly. Nothing could break us.

Debbie thanked me for the fantastic party and gifts. Noah left us alone for our girls' night, understanding that Debbie needed me, and went to bed.

A week passed, and everything was going well. I was grateful that my morning sickness had stopped. At work, I had a difficult customer, and though I wanted to chop off her dry hair, I did my job professionally, rolling my eyes in frustration.

The new employees were doing well, and I was heading home when my cell phone rang. Debbie needed a ride to the hospital. I rushed to her cabin, where she was waiting, clearly in pain.

I helped Debbie into the car and called Noah to meet us at the hospital. Debbie urged me to hurry, but I kept my pace steady to avoid an accident.

"We're ten minutes away, don't worry. The babies will be okay," I reassured her as she sobbed.

"I'm scared, Nicole," she said.

"I know you are," I replied.

At the hospital, I called for a nurse, who brought a wheelchair and took Debbie to a room. I followed them, my phone ringing with a call from Fany, a customer complaining about the new girl being rude and not knowing what she needed. *Gosh!* Rolling my eyes, I hung up, realizing I probably lost a customer. But I had more important things to focus on.

I ran back to hold Debbie's hand as she endured the pain like a champ. I was so proud of her.

Each hour, Debbie grew weaker. I gave her ice chips, wiped her forehead with a cold towel, and kept encouraging her.

Finally, the doctor said, "You are fully dilated."

They gave me a gown, and half an hour later, the twins were born. Two tiny boys. Debbie held them and turned to me with a smile and tears in her eyes.

"What are their names?" I asked.

"Asher and Aaron. They'll take my last name, John," she answered, exhausted.

"Well, Debbie John, you did an awesome job!" I said, beaming.

Noah and I went to see the babies. They were adorable. We let Debbie rest and decided to come back the next morning. I took pictures of Asher and Aaron. The nurse asked if I wanted to hold one of the babies, and that's when I knew just how much I wanted to be a mom. Noah held the other twin, and it didn't matter which one we had in our arms.

We saw Debbie sleeping, left flowers in a vase, and went home to take Maxwell for a walk. Noah had to cover a night shift for a coworker, so I watched the Food Channel with Maxwell by my side. It was a good end to a fabulous day.

Chapter 6

Tough Pregnancy

I felt grateful that my pregnancy was coming along well. It was such a blessing to feel my tummy growing, though in the back of my mind, I was scared of losing another baby. I didn't feel strong enough to go through that again.

Watching Debbie be a single mom made me so proud of her. I tried to help with the baby boys, even though I kept mixing up their names. They were identical after all, and it always made us laugh. Drake didn't want anything to do with the boys, but he was paying child support. Debbie planned to find a babysitter, maybe her mother, so she could return to work. For now, she was enjoying her bundle of joy.

As the days went by, I gained weight, and I was happy. Noah took good care of me, talking to my tummy and even singing songs. I felt spoiled. One day, during a walk, I started getting cramps. Noah rushed me to the emergency room.

"You'll be fine, don't worry," he said.

The doctor told me everything was fine but to stay in bed for two weeks. I was okay with that and stopped eating spicy foods because heartburn was uncomfortable. I stayed in bed watching the Food Network, reading baby books, and resting as the doctor ordered. Noah cooked dinner and walked Maxwell.

After the two weeks, things went back to normal. Debbie was back at work, and everything felt ordinary again.

Debbie and I went out for lunch, and she showed me pictures of the baby boys. Her mother was staying with them. "How are you doing, Nicole?" she asked in a worried voice.

"I'm terrific, no worries. Everything is coming along fine. Thank goodness Noah has been wonderful," I told her.

I was grateful to have a best friend to talk to besides my husband. My craving for pickles and vanilla ice cream was overwhelming but so good. I loved being pregnant, but I hoped I didn't gain too much weight.

One day, there was a knock at the door, and to my surprise, my mother-in-law stood there, with flowers, a gallon of ice cream, and a jar of pickles.

"Noah told me about your cravings, so…" She smiled awkwardly as she handed me the goodies. "I came to apologize for how I treated you last time I was here. You are a strong, loving woman, and I'm proud of you and grateful you are my daughter-in-law," she said.

We sobbed together as she apologized. We were no longer rivals… but a family.

My mother-in-law made me lunch, and we ate together. When she left, I felt hopeful that our family would be getting along now. Families are there to support and love each other. Whoever said you married the family too was right.

I felt tired, so I read a book in bed with Maxwell. Noah had the night shift, which was okay with me. I needed rest and silence, handling my pregnancy with care. I couldn't bear to lose another baby. It was always on my mind, and I know it was only natural to feel this way after what we've been through.

By the seventh month, the doctors said I had to stop working and stay in bed most of the time, trying to stay stress-free. Debbie planned a baby shower for me next Saturday, and I called Maria to clean the house and make me dinner for four days. She loved to cook, and I liked watching her prepare fresh veggies and make homemade corn tortillas.

A week passed quickly, and I prepared for my baby shower. My tummy was small, but we were excited to learn at the last appointment that it was a baby boy. We wanted to be parents.

I put my brown hair in a nice ponytail and wore a simple blue dress. Noah took photos of family and friends playing baby games and eating the cute blue sandwiches. I made sure not to stress about anything.

Debbie brought the boys, and Noah took the twins out back so she could have fun. I would never forget this day—unwrapping gifts, laughing, and being so happy. It felt like a new chapter of life. The whole day was a success, with fantastic gifts and many photos for the album. Life was good. The house was messy, but that was okay.

Noah took Debbie and the boys home while I threw all the wrapping paper in the trash, watched television, and waited for Noah. He took two hours, which I found odd since he never stayed that long. I heard the car park in the driveway.

"Hey, you're still up? The boys were cranky, so I stayed to help Debbie until they fell asleep," he explained.

"Well, that was nice of you. It's sad they don't have a dad to love or care for them," I said, feeling exhausted.

On my eighth month, I was ready to have my baby boy. My legs were swollen, and I was wobbling everywhere, craving tacos and fried foods. I didn't care. One more month, and my baby would be in my arms. Maria cleaned the cabin, made Mexican food, and helped me decorate the baby's room. I painted trees and baby animals on the wall. It was so colorful, with flowers and birds beautifully added with the paintbrush. Noah took me to a romantic restaurant with candlelight. He drank wine while I drank milk.

"I am so in love with you. I will love you forever, Nicole," he whispered in my ear.

"And I'll love you forever and ever, Noah," I replied. We embraced.

We went home and cuddled all night. I had never been so happy. Maxwell joined us, and his loud snoring was comical. Everything was perfect, but in the back of my mind, I feared it was the calm before the storm. Waiting for something to happen was scary... no one is this happy without something going wrong.

Chapter 7

Snowy Night

My water broke in the middle of the night. The pain worsened quickly. Noah was coming from work, which wasn't far, and so I got ready, grabbed my small suitcase, and sat on the couch. With the pain getting stronger, Noah helped me into the car and rushed to the hospital. But I felt like I wasn't going to make it.

"Noah! Stop the car and help me! I feel the baby's head," I cried.

"Okay, sweetheart." He laid a blanket on the snow and told me to lie down.

Noah checked me and said, "You're right. The baby is ready to be born. Push, Nicole, push again."

I watched the night sky and the snow coming down as our baby boy was born. His cries were like music to my ears. I had never been so grateful in my whole life. I wanted to reach out to Grandpa Buck to say, "I'm a mother now."

Noah wrapped our bundle of joy in a blanket and drove us to the hospital. It snowed all night, and they finally brought my baby back into my arms once again. We had decided on his name not so long ago. *Andy.* His fair skin, dark hair and blue eyes were perfect as he played with his hands.

"Who does he look like, you or me?" Noah asked, beaming like the proud dad that he was.

"Of course, his daddy," I said with a smile. We were so grateful to God for the beautiful gift.

Debbie arrived with the loveliest flowers. She carried Andy and said, "He is so handsome. The girls will be all over this little boy."

"Let me enjoy my baby boy before you make him eighteen."

We laughed.

"Where are your twins, Debbie?" I asked.

"They're with Mother. She spoils those boys. I called Maria so she could help with the baby for a couple of days. You'll thank me later," she giggled.

We took our bundle of joy home, and I still had to pinch myself to believe this was real. My dream had come true. I was a mother and would try my best to be an excellent mommy to Andy.

The first week was a breeze. He only cried when he was hungry. I couldn't stop staring at him. He was so cute with his big blue eyes, just like his father. Noah would sing to him, and their bond was lovely to see. We were fortunate that Noah's family was coming to stay for two days. Maria was a great help, but I had to look for a babysitter, which worried me. I had two months to decide what to do. Maria wanted to make fried food, so I told her no more fried food.

"I've got to watch my weight," I said.

Maria smiled and said, "That's why I don't have a husband. I like being chunky." She patted me on the shoulder, laughing.

She tossed a fabulous salad and let me take a nap.

Life was good.

Andy was now one month old. I watched his every move with a smile that lightened my heart. He was the love of my life, and he was growing fast. I told him every day, "I will love you forever."

Noah kissed me, took the baby in his arms, sang him a lullaby, and put him to sleep. He was so good with Andy… a perfect daddy.

I had to find a daycare soon as I needed to go back to work. I had three places I was looking into.

By the second month, I felt great. I went to a doctor's appointment and checked out the beauty salon. Debbie and the girls hovered over Andy. If I say so myself, he was adorable, being his mother and all. I hugged everyone and went home. I was tired… it had been a long day and Andy was getting cranky. He wanted to be home in his crib, surrounded by familiar things. I felt the same way.

Monday was the first day without my baby boy. Noah and I took Andy to daycare. They greeted us and took the baby from my arms. It felt like they were taking my whole life away. I kissed him and told him I would return in a few hours, though it felt like forever.

Chapter 8

The Unthinkable

We had gotten used to our routine for the past two weeks, and everything flowed perfectly. Today, I was late. I took Andy to the daycare, kissed him on the forehead, and his giggle made me pause for a minute. Life was perfect, and my baby boy made me feel happy.

After leaving him, my day turned horrible. The customers were mean and awful, and all I could think about was Andy giggling. Then I heard a shout. Margaret, a customer, was crying because I had cut her hair short.

"I will sue you for cutting my long hair," she roared.

"You told me to cut the length!" I screamed back.

Debbie took me to the office and dealt with the problem. The day felt so long that I just wanted to pick up Andy and go home, but I continued with my day.

It was almost closing time when I got a phone call from the daycare. I grabbed my purse and rushed to the car, driving two miles like a crazy woman. When I arrived, I saw Noah and the paramedics. He was carrying Andy, trying to revive him, but it was no use. Our baby was pronounced dead. He had vomited and choked.

I fell to my knees. Noah brought Andy to me and put him in my arms. I rocked him for an hour, not wanting to let him go. I kissed him and whispered, "I love you forever." Over and over. But he could no longer hear.

When they finally took him from my arms, I had cried a river. It felt like my tears would never stop.

We don't know why things happen. All I knew was that my son was gone, and it could have been prevented. I had felt something was wrong that day, but life got in the way. I should never have left him at that place. I blamed myself for Andy's death.

I remembered the night Andy was born and how quickly I bonded with him. My heart had been bursting with love and joy, looking at his precious face, his little fingers wrapped around mine. I had never felt more wanted, needed, and gratified. I knew then that I would take care of him because he was the center of my universe. But now… he was just… gone.

Debbie took me home, and I went to bed, sobbing for our loss. My best friend stayed with me until Noah came home, and I heard them whispering.

"What happened to Andy?" Debbie asked.

"They gave him a bottle with a pillow and left him alone. He choked on his vomit," Noah replied.

He wept, and Debbie hugged him while I lay in the room, hearing about my son's last moments. *This was unthinkable. Why was my son dead?*

I fell asleep exhausted. That night, it rained, with menacing clouds and lightning. I felt numb and empty.

"You left us with a broken heart. That day came way too quickly, and my tears gush like a river with love and anger. When it's all said and done, we will love you forever, my precious Andy. You were our light, the love that lit up our hearts and lives. Our hearts are broken without you. I can't bear our days and nights without you, Son. Our life is now a tale of misery. Nothing could prepare me to lose you—the pain of losing you is unbearable, and I cannot be strong enough to endure your loss. You were a gift from God, and there's no substitute for you. There are no more giggles and smiles. I know you're gone forever, but you'll be forever in my heart. I console myself by remembering all the love we shared. I wake up with an empty, shattered heart every day and it will never be whole again. We miss you, my little Andy. Our few memories are not enough, and three months wasn't enough. Meanwhile, we'll wait to join you, Son… wait for us."

Making the funeral arrangements was difficult. I needed help even bathing myself. Noah was there for me. Maria helped clean the cabin, and I was grateful. I told her to leave the baby's room alone. I fell into a deep slumber.

"Grandpa Buck, what are you doing here?"

"My dear, you are going to be okay. Life throws curveballs. Your son is in Heaven, so don't worry, sweetheart. You will soon be with your baby boy. The time here is different. It's like a blink of an eye for us, though it has been years for you. Love you forever."

I awoke sobbing. I couldn't believe I had dreamt about Grandpa Buck. I missed him so much. The reality of my son being gone made me retreat into despair.

Noah was at work and came home smelling like liquor. This was tough for him, but we didn't say a word to each other. The grieving process was lonely and dark. I was starting not to care.

We couldn't ignore each other forever. We blamed ourselves for Andy being gone, but how do we make the pain disappear?

Maxwell was barking, but I wanted to sleep. I had been taking sleeping pills because the nights were scary. I kept hearing Andy crying for me.

Chapter 9

The Aftermath

We took a seat in the small chapel. The coffin was so tiny, and the thought of Andy being alone in it broke my heart. Noah held me tightly, as if I would break apart any moment. He could be right. Everyone was silent. Debbie sat next to us, holding my hand.

The pastor began the service, but all I could hear were people murmuring, "I'm sorry." It felt like I was outside my body, shutting everyone out, unable to concentrate on the service. The flowers smelled lovely—blue roses—but the day was unbearably long. I just wanted to hide from everyone.

Grandpa Buck used to say you could hide, but the problem would still be there tomorrow. Conquer issues today because you might not have that chance tomorrow.

I told Debbie I needed to go home. If I heard another "sorry," I might vomit.

"Are you sure? What about Noah?" she asked.

"Noah is okay with his parents and friends."

I took Maxwell for a walk. The poor thing had only heard me sobbing for days. Noah called to say he was going to his parents' house, which was fine with me. We all heal differently.

The next day, I wasn't feeling well. I realized I hadn't eaten the day before, so I made myself some toast—it was all I could manage. My stomach protested, but after feeling a bit better, I showered and drove to Debbie's house. I needed some girl time and wanted to see her twin boys. Everything was so quiet. Maybe they were napping. I didn't want to knock and wake the boys, so I got the key from under the mat, quietly opened the door, and walked toward her bedroom.

When I opened the door, my jaw dropped in shock. Noah and Debbie were having sex. Their faces were priceless.

I ran out of her house as fast as I could and fell to my knees, hearing Noah call after me to wait. There was nothing to say. The man I loved, and my best friend were together. I couldn't even comprehend what was happening.

I needed to be alone, so I decided to leave for Hawaii. I packed my suitcase, took money from the cookie jar, and got a flight. Even though I wasn't feeling well, I needed to be on the beach and take a week to think about what to do next.

This pain on top of my grief was double agony. I couldn't get the image of the two of them together out of my head. The good thing was I was wearing my sunglasses, which I wanted to break. Debbie had given them to me last Christmas—that bitch. *How long had the affair been going on?*

At some point, I fell asleep. The noise of people talking and leaving the airplane woke me. I got my suitcase and went on my way. I called for an Uber, which took me to a condo right by the beach. Once I was rested, I went to the beach, read a book, and in between chapters, watched the waves.

I took a peek at my cell phone. There were so many texts and voicemails from Debbie and Noah. I didn't want to deal with them or their lies.

Chapter 10

Forgiveness

I dressed for dinner, listened to music, and took a night stroll. Tears flowed at some point, reminding me I would soon have to face the reality of my broken life. Three days flew by like the wind on a cold day. With two more days of paradise left, I went hiking but felt ill and fainted. I woke up in a nearby hospital, listening to the beeping of machines. Dr. Iwalani Chow came in, concerned, and wanted to run more tests. I gave my permission to proceed.

The following morning, he returned with news that shook my world. Stage four cancer in my pelvis. I couldn't believe what I was hearing. He advised me to return home and see my doctor for treatment. I explained that I had already undergone chemotherapy for breast cancer and didn't want to go through it again.

I booked a flight home and called my doctor, who wanted to see me immediately. My tears wouldn't stop flowing as I returned to Big Bear. I rushed to my doctor's appointment for a second opinion.

"I wish I had better news," he said. "You have stage four cancer, and it has spread to other parts of your body. I'm so sorry, Nicole. You probably have two weeks to three months. There's nothing we can do but keep you comfortable with meds. I don't recommend chemo."

"Thanks for everything, doctor," I replied, my voice low. What was there to say?

"Spend time with your family and friends."

I nodded... when what I really wanted to do was scream.

I walked to my car, sobbing, and a kind man helped me into my vehicle. They weren't kidding—life is short. I knew I had to wrap up my life, and I would start by forgiving Noah and Debbie.

Noah was waiting for me at home. Maxwell jumped on me with excitement, making me giggle. "I missed you too, boy."

I turned to Noah, preparing myself to tell him the news.

"Noah, I have to tell you something."

"You already know that Debbie is pregnant?" he blurted out.

I paused, catching my breath and bearings. It felt like a stab in the back, but it didn't matter now. After taking a few deep breaths, I said, "No, I didn't know you two were having a baby. Well, my news comes at the right time. Before anything else, I just want you to know that I love you forever, Noah."

"What news?" he asked, looking ashamed.

"They gave me three months to live. The cancer is back. It's stage four this time."

Noah ran to embrace me, and we cried, letting out all the despair, the sadness, and the hopelessness. Despite everything, I still loved him and always would. Nothing else mattered. I wanted him to be happy. I didn't have much time, but I wanted to spend my last days with Noah, and he agreed. He kept apologizing for his affair with my best friend.

I wasn't ready to talk to Debbie, so she stayed away. I instructed my lawyer to come over for my will and testament, giving my business to Debbie and the cabin to Noah.

Each day, I grew weaker, and Maxwell moaned, sensing my decline, perhaps. Noah and I went camping, and Maxwell was thrilled with that. It was the ending I had hoped for in my life. We didn't go far—just under the stars with a full moon. It was divine.

Knowing my time was running out, I told Noah to call Debbie when we got home. It was time for forgiveness.

Lying in bed, I heard a knock and said, "Come in."

"Hey, how are you feeling?" Debbie asked tentatively, not knowing what to say.

"I'm doing okay," I answered. *Never better,* I thought, chuckling to myself.

She ran to my side, knelt by my bed, and broke down. "I'm so sorry I hurt you. There are no excuses for what I did," she sobbed as she held my hand.

"Let me talk. I have little time. Debbie, I forgive you and Noah. I want you to know that and find peace. I'm glad he won't be alone and will have a family with you. Make him happy. I wish you the best, my friend. I love you."

We sobbed together. I told her to call Noah. He came in and lay on the bed. Debbie left the room, and the love of my life held me until my heart's last beat.

My story ended there, but Noah's life began anew. I walked the steps of Heaven with my baby boy Andy and Grandpa Buck.

We are only here for a moment, and then the wind blows, and we are gone.

Life is a gift. We should live as if there is no tomorrow.

I had a great life, and found love… and I will love Noah forever.

No regrets.

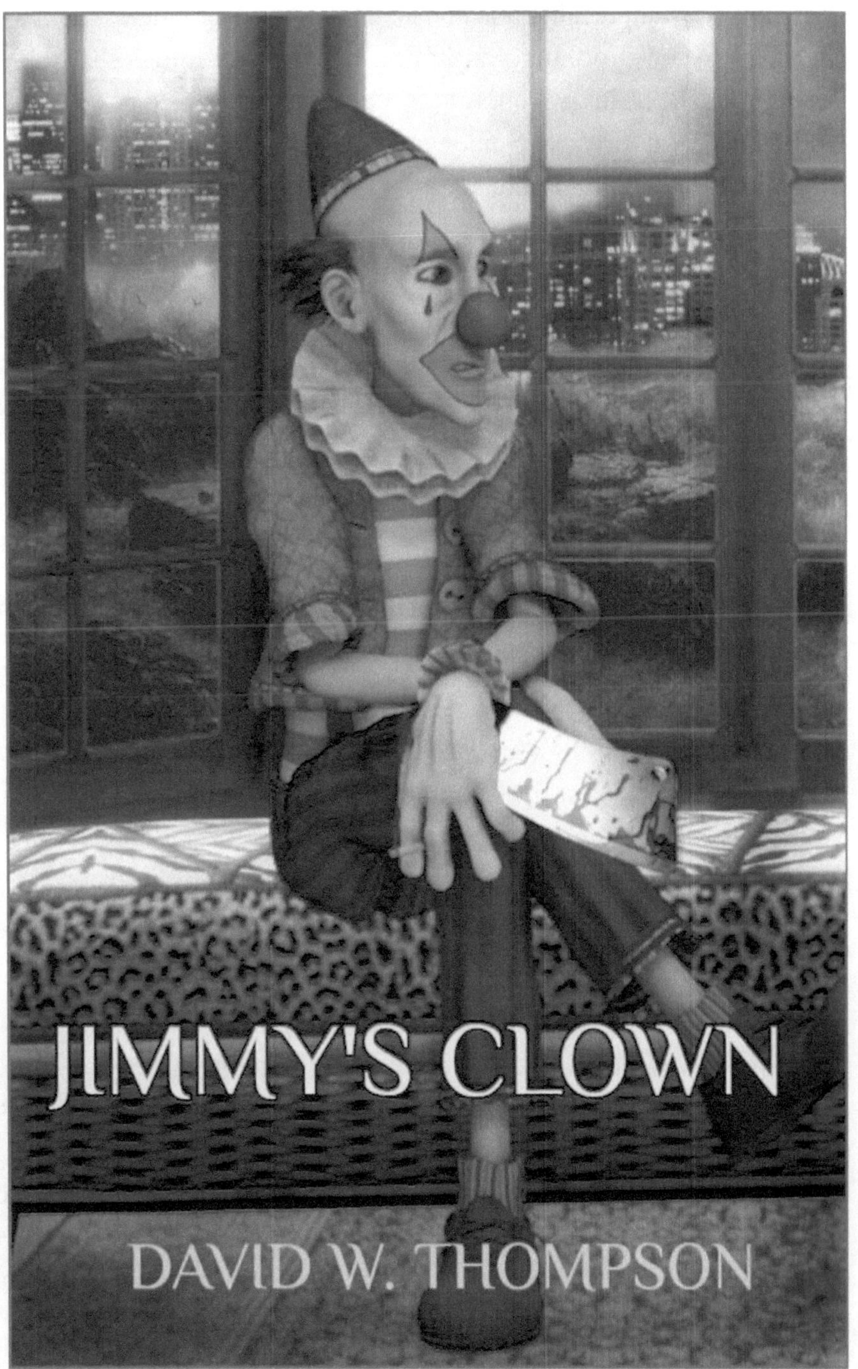
JIMMY'S CLOWN
DAVID W. THOMPSON

It was tough having an older brother as a kid. A typical week included constant teasing and slaps on the back of my head when Mom and Dad weren't looking and hiding my favorite things. Some days, Jimmy was unusually creative, like putting itch powder in my underwear…my favorite Spider-Man ones, too. But it was my brother who did all the complaining… about me.

"I hate staying home to *baby*sit you, punk," he'd say.

"Why do you follow me around like an unwanted puppy?"

If I so much as sniffled when he snatched my arm behind my back or twisted my ears, it was: "Oh, is the poor "wittle" baby gonna cry? Poor Sammy."

Jimmy was six years older (and he'd say wiser), but that gave him the advantage. He was bigger, stronger, and meaner—mostly meaner…

I got my revenge when and where I could. My successes resulted in arm twists or a very public wedgie, compliments of Jimmy.

When my brother was fifteen years old, he discovered girls. I caught him researching "How to pick up girls" and "What girls look for in a boyfriend" on the computer. I teased him about it but didn't squeal about the dog-eared magazines he kept hidden under his mattress. I was saving that information for a special occasion. When Becky Fay's family moved into a house on our cul-de-sac, it was a matter of time before he made a fool of himself…and I planned to witness it.

Jimmy didn't waste any time. The schools were out for the summer, so getting acquainted there was impossible. That didn't stop Jimmy. He stalked her as I watched from my bedroom window. He walked past her house to a small grove of trees, stood behind an old oak, and waited. Did I mention Jimmy wasn't very creative? He was off to the races when he spotted her blonde ponytail bobbing down their driveway to the mailbox.

Becky must've been desperate for teenage companionship, and Jimmy hoped to claim her as his own before school resumed. The first Saturday after the family moved in, he was invited to their pool.

Jimmy was up early that Saturday, although his pool date wasn't until noon. Mom called us to breakfast and delivered the bad news…bad for Jimmy anyway.

"Jimmy, your dad and I were called in to work today. You'll need to watch your brother until we get back."

"But, Mom, I have plans."

"You can cancel them, or you can take your brother along. That's up to you, but it will be good for you both to spend some quality time together; you're always picking on him."

("Quality time" with Jimmy. I'd have to remember that one when our English teacher asked for examples of an oxymoron again.)

"But why do I get stuck with the little brat?" Jimmy protested.

"Because I said so. We must go to work. If you have anything else to say, you can spend the rest of the summer complaining about it and reading in your room."

***

Becky answered the door on the first knock and welcomed us in. One thing about Jimmy is that he had good taste. Becky was a lovely girl—inside and out. Her bright blue eyes sparkled when she laughed…and she laughed often, but not in a silly, giggly teenage girl way.

"Would you fine gents like a cola? There's some in the fridge. Sweet tea, too, if you'd like."

"I'd like a sweet tea if it isn't too much trouble, Becky," I said as Jimmy stared ahead, tongue-tied.

Becky led us to the living room to have our drinks. Jimmy sipped on his cola, which she assumed was his choice, given his silence. He avoided eye contact with her, staring at the floor, walls, and ceiling instead. I had to bite my lip to conceal a smile.

Jimmy stood up and stepped toward Becky on the couch. I thought he would sit beside her for a moment, but he reached to a shelf behind her instead. He grabbed a large figurine and held it up for me to see. A scaly hell demon with glowing red eyes glared back at me. I couldn't stop the shudder that began at the base of my spine and shot upwards.

"Here's one my little brother will like, Becky. He's scared of everything: ghouls and ghosts, witches and warlocks, vamps and werewolves—you name it. Everything gives him nightmares."

I wasn't surprised that an opportunity to demean me would bring Jimmy out of his shell, but he picked on the wrong little brother this time. I sucked in a breath of air, reached out, and took the demon figure from him. My hand shook, but Becky didn't seem to notice.

"This is a scary-looking demon, but not everything scares me, Jimmy... clowns, for instance," I said, placing it back on the shelf. "Why don't you tell Becky why we can't go to the neighborhood burger joint?"

Jimmy's face flushed, and the pimples he'd carefully covered with makeup (which he called medicine) popped out a brilliant red.

"I'll tell you why. There's a clown in the place," I answered. "Clowns terrorize Jimmy, yup, even burger clowns."

"What?" Becky laughed. "You can't be serious? Jimmy? Really?"

I thought Jimmy's face was as red as possible; now, it looked like his skin was on fire.

"Sorry," he mumbled and took off down the hall. He didn't stop running until he was home with a heavy oak door between him and his shame.

I enjoyed the afternoon with Becky, even though I knew I'd pay for it later. I told my parents I got the black eye and split lip from tripping on the stairs.

***

For several years following the episode at Becky's, things got worse with my brother. One night, thumbtacks were left in my bed. The following week, it was a nest of cockroaches. My homework was destroyed. A note was sent to my teacher threatening her. It was signed with an autograph that looked like mine but was not. That one got me suspended.

As I grew, Jimmy's bullying diminished for a while, but the scars remained. He could still overpower me, but not without some consequence to himself.

My parents had a birthday party for Jimmy when he turned eighteen. One of his friends, Daniel, had a sister I was sweet on. Daniel didn't like me and wasted little time showing me. He pantsed me in front of everyone, even the girls. Jimmy joined in on the "fun," and I ran to the woods, my refuge. The two of them and several others joined in the chase. I ran as fast as my legs would carry me. Deeper and deeper into the woods, into an area I'd never been to. As I ran, the catcalls and the mock howling faded.

When I couldn't hear them anymore, I turned to retrace my steps. Every footfall was placed with care. I planned to return to familiar woods and wait for the creeps to go home before doing the same. I had no desire to be discovered before then.

The further I walked, the more lost I became in the moonless night. The calls of nocturnal creatures and the sound of passing footsteps only made it scarier. Owls screeched, and foxes yelped in concert with other sounds I was afraid to label. Sleep didn't come easy that night. It was the night my nightmares began.

The nightly terrors are always the same. A stranger is walking down a wooded lane. I'm above the man, watching from the branches of a tall tree. A classic clown figure follows him, matching him step by step. The clown is garishly dressed in huge yellow shoes, an orange plaid shirt with purple-striped baggy pants, and a red rubber nose.

165

As the stranger speeds up, the clown does, too. When the stranger begins to run, the clown hits the gas, gaining on him. The stranger runs faster and faster, branches snapping, briars clawing at his clothes. Ten yards from a well-traveled road and his hope for safety, a dirty, white-gloved hand reaches out, pulls him back into the brush, and…

The ending is never good—not for the stranger. Sometimes, he survives with a missing limb or broken bones. Other times, he is not so lucky. The dream has haunted me for years, and I seldom experience a peaceful night. Even after moving into my new home, the dreams persist. However, the main character in my dreams has changed. He isn't so strange anymore; he is always someone I know well. The dream feels increasingly real with each passing night, and I wake up choking back a scream every morning. I'm unsure what's happening to me. One morning, I discovered a red-stained white glove under my pillow. How did it get there? Who put it there?

Last night's dream was the worst. I dreamt of Jimmy. I cannot describe the disgust…the horror. This time, I came down from my perch in the trees. The clown welcomed me to the thrill of the chase… My dream self aching again for the coppery taste of blood!

When it was done, I shook myself awake and went to the bathroom to wash my face. It took some scrubbing to remove the white grease paint. The yellow floppy shoes I keep tucked away in my closet? They're ruined. I'll never get the blood stains out.

Jimmy doesn't have to be afraid of clowns…not anymore.

Revenge is indeed a rare dish. And it's delicious served hot or cold.

EYE of the
JAGUAR
Robert Allen Lupton

Martina Crestada focused her binoculars and looked down into the cenote, one of the sinkholes riddling the karst landscape of the Yucatan peninsula. The building storm clouds scuttled across the face of the moon making it flicker like a guttering candle.

"Philip, hold the flashlight still, this one isn't filled with water and there's a carved altar stone in the center."

He balanced his flashlight on the cenote's rim to steady it. Philip lived to make Martina happy. While he'd become fascinated with Mesoamerican history and lore, his love of Martina was the primary reason he'd majored in Mayan culture and the only reason he'd joined this archeological expedition.

"Martina, we'd best hurry, the clouds are building. I smell rain and we're an hour from camp. It's dangerous at night. Ocelots, jaguars, and wolves, oh my!"

Martina pointed her flashlight upward from under her chin ensuring Philip could see her look of disgust. "Don't be a crybaby. I see an altar stone on the bottom. There's writing, but I can't read it. Red veins. Could be iron oxide. Maybe blood. How exciting! Philip, I hope they're bloodstains!"

"I'll record the GPS reading and tell the guide we're ready to leave. We'll come back tomorrow."

The guide screamed. He pointed at a jaguar skulking quietly as a gentle breeze and shouted *"B'alam! B'alam!"* The beast moved nearer the explorers and pinned them against the pit's edge. Philip was unarmed, he had a flashlight, a pocketknife, and a pith helmet like the explorers wear in a Tarzan movie.

The jaguar's eyes glowed like red coals. Philip froze in place. The cat charged without warning and Philip threw his helmet like a flying disk and hit the jaguar in the shoulder. He shoved Martina to one side and stepped backward away from the leaping cat. He struggled futilely for purchase on the crumbling pit edge. He fell into the cenote and the jaguar flew over his head and into the pit with him. They both screamed all the way down.

Philip woke up on the decayed leaves that dotted the altar stone. He felt his left arm. *Shit, broken. Dark down here. Where's my damn flashlight?"*

Martina shouted, "Philip!"

"I'm alive. Broken, but alive."

"I'll send the guide for help."

"Have them bring a harness. Pretty sure my arm is broken. I can't climb out. The air is stale, and it stinks of rotten fruit."

"Is the jaguar, or should I say, the B'alam, dead? We can practice speaking Mayan until help comes."

Philip found his flashlight. The jaguar draped the altar stone like a praying supplicant. Chiseled images of cats, snakes, and wolves appeared and vanished with the sweeping of the flashlight's beam. Philip crept slowly to the jaguar and gently touched its throat seeking a pulse.

The creature opened its eyes, snarled, and bit Philip's arm. He tried to jerk away and cursed. "Christ, damn thing bit me. Probably has rabies!" He searched the altar with his free hand, the one attached to a broken arm. He caught a brief vision of an obsidian knife stored in a cubbyhole. He gritted his teeth against the pain, stretched for the knife, and stabbed the jaguar in the neck. The creature released his arm. He wiggled the knife until the glow in the beast's eyes faded to darkness. Their blood mingled and flowed into the red-stained cracks atop the limestone altar. The stench of rotted fruit grew overpowering. Philip couldn't breathe, he gasped, staggered back from the altar, his head spun, and he passed out.

The pain from the jaguar bite or his broken arm woke him. Flickering torchlight and rancid smoke filled the cenote. Several men, costumed in ancient Mayan ceremonial regalia, filled the cavern. He shouted for Martina. She didn't answer, but above him, the pit's edge was lined with women and children.

The quiet was frightening. It was like the silent moment in a horror film before all hell breaks loose. Philip remembered from a class on negotiation that the person who speaks first, loses. He couldn't stand it. The people just stared at him.

He spoke in English. "I didn't know you were filming a movie. I'm sorry if I messed up the take. I need help. I'm bleeding and I think my arm is broken."

A short ugly tattooed man with a feathered headdress and bad teeth waved an obsidian knife and spoke in Mayan. His pronunciation and cadence were understandable, but different than what Philip had learned in class. "Who are you? Why you here? You dare disturb our sacred ceremony! You killed B'alam, the symbol of life, and you flaunt your evildoing by displaying his body on the gateway altar to Xibalba, the underworld. The gods are angry."

A snake tattoo on the man's sweat-covered forearm writhed in the torchlight. Philip said, "Where's the camera? I said I'm sorry. I'll pay for any damage to your set, but I'm really hurting here. I need a doctor. Please stop with the Hollywood Mayan mumbo jumbo and help me."

Snake Tattoo pointed at Philip and intoned to his congregation, "Bitten by B'alam. Their blood is mingled." He motioned to a larger man, who stepped forward and punched Philip in the stomach with a wooden club. It knocked the wind out of him. Philip bent over and the man clubbed him in the head.

The second time Philip woke in the cenote he was tied spread-eagled on the altar. Still no Martina, but his audience was mostly visible through the smoke and fumes. Women dressed in traditional tunics, the huipil, flitted like shadows in dissipating fog. They moved quickly, but as silently as hungry herons seeking food on the misty bayou morning. They were visible and then they weren't. The smoke slowly rose out of the cenote, and he saw several women around him. One with a tattooed face, turquoise earrings, and a traje, a colorful dress that reached to her sandals, turned his head from side to side. Her sash, the faja, was ornately beaded. The other women carried small clay pots and slivers of obsidian. He was truly frightened. Who were these people?

Snake Tattoo said, "The gods demand we sacrifice this strangely clothed man. His sacrilege is an affront to Xibalba and his murder of the B'alam insults all gods. The afterlife is now closed to us and only his death will reopen the pathway. He's unclean and unworthy to share blood with the B'alam. He's pale and ugly and must be made pleasing in the eyes of Itzamna, the god who rules all gods. Itzamna demands a worthy sacrifice."

The women forced a disgusting herbal mixture down his throat. It tasted of rotting mushrooms and stank of old blood. The ancient Mayan priests made a psychotropic potion from mushrooms, lilies, and toad sweat. He gagged at the thought of toad sweat and vomited. The woman in the faja turned his head to one side and other women caught his vomit in clay bowls ensuring that he didn't foul the altar. They pinched his nose and filled his mouth with tea made from cascara bark. The tea and psychotropic purgative flushed his body from both ends.

Once his spasms stopped, the women washed him. He tried to fight but was too weak from the purgative and emetic to put up much resistance. One pressed his broken arm. Philip screamed in pain, but he stopped fighting.

They held him tighter than the ropes binding him, chanted in unison, and stabbed him rhythmically with sharp obsidian splinters they dipped into the ink-filled pots. The women worked in relays and covered his entire body with tattoos. The pain was relentless.

The women worked faster than modern sewing machines. Dip the obsidian needle in ink, tap the splinter with a stone hammer to embed the ink beneath his skin, and repeat about thirty times a minute. His body bled from a thousand cuts. He squirmed and he screamed, but the women never broke rhythm.

Philip woke and passed out, and he woke and passed out again. He was dehydrated and weak from the forced bouts of diarrhea and vomiting, but the tattooing continued unabated. Sometimes daylight was visible above the cenote and sometimes it wasn't, but there were always people watching from overhead. He was groggy and never entirely awake or asleep. On the fourth, or maybe the fifth day, the women tattooed his groin area, and any residual hope he had that this was a dream, or that he'd fallen into a movie set was dispelled when the relentless obsidian needles moved from his upper thigh. He clenched his teeth so hard that he broke two of them.

Mercifully, the women finally finished. A single ray of moonlight, like a tangible beam, gleamed from the full clear sky. His audience waited, quiet and expectant. The now familiar scent of rotten fruit filled the air, and it was stronger and more pungent than ever. His flesh was raw and sore from his new tattoos and hand-braided hemp ropes felt like white-hot branding irons against his flesh.

The priest covered him with the skin of the jaguar he'd killed and lifted an obsidian knife overhead. The smoke from the fruit incense made Philip's head spin. He tried to move, but his muscles wouldn't respond. His eyes locked open in terror and the knife descended. The priest dropped the knife. "His eyes," he screamed. "He has B'alam's eyes. The god lives within him."

Philip strained against his ropes and one blood-slicken arm slid free. He stared at his arm. Brownish orange and white fur sprouted through the snake tattoo covering his right arm from wrist to shoulder. He untied one of his fur-covered legs. He reached for the other, but his hands had become claws. He slit his bindings with a sharp talon.

Philip rolled from the altar, stood on four feet, and swished his tail from side to side. Philip stalked toward the now supplicant priest and sniffed. The man, like a martyr, stank of fear and rapture. Philip nosed the man's face and locked eyes with him. The priest shouted. "B'alam lives in this man. Ware his eyes when the moon comes full. Death lives in his eyes. Mighty B'alam, have mercy on your servant."

Philip tore off the priest's head with the swipe of a single claw and fed on him. The people watching from the rim of the cenote danced and cheered.

The next morning a shout from the cenote's edge woke Philip. He wiped the clotted blood from his face. The voice continued. "You are blessed by B'alam to be the embodiment of the god on earth. Command us as you will."

"Get me the hell out of this damn pit."

The Mayans lowered a long ladder. Philip climbed about halfway up and felt compelled to go back down. He retrieved the obsidian knife and returned it to the cubbyhole.

A woman brought him a bowl of clean water and he washed. His reflection was jarring. His countenance bore a bluish-green tattoo of a jaguar's face, and his eyes, his eyes were the slitted eyes of a jungle cat. He rinsed the blood from his arms and legs. It hadn't been a dream. He was tattooed everywhere.

Philip rested and thought for three days. He was in human form, but he remembered being a jaguar. Was he a were-jaguar? Was there even such a thing" He called the Mayan leaders. "I will sleep alone every night in the cenote. No one is permitted there. When the full moon is in the sky, I will take the ladder down with me."

"As B'alam commands."

"During the days you will carve messages onto large stones. I will compose the messages and you will carve them."

"It shall be done."

Eleven months later, Philip and the stonemasons finished the last stone's inscription. Philip considered signing it, but he didn't. He inspected the row of Mayan Rosetta stones. Two languages side by side, Mayan and Spanish. *Wonder how the professors will like this*, he thought. "Lower the stones into the pit and bury them near the altar," he told the men. "The moon is full tonight. I hunger and require a human sacrifice. Select one wisely."

The new priest said, "We've got the man. He murdered his neighbor for the want of his wife."

At sunset, Philip and the murderer climbed down the ladder. Philip ordered, "Take up the ladder. Leave this area and never return."

The ladder vanished. Philip tied the murderer to the altar and waited for the moonrise. *The mixture of human and jaguar blood opened some sort of portal once before, perhaps it will again.*

The moon rose and fur sprouted on Philp's arms. Before his hands became paws, he sliced his palm with the obsidian knife and returned it to its hiding place. He told the murderer that he was sorry. Philip's mouth grew fangs, and he tore the man's neck open. Philip clenched his paw-like fist and squeezed. His blood mingled with the murderer's and dripped onto the altar stone. The stench of rotted fruit bloomed inside the cenote and Philip passed out.

***

A hand touched Philip's face and he snapped, catching it with his teeth. He tasted blood and opened his eyes. Martina's face was above him. She shouted, "I found him. He's alive." She jerked her hand free, put it in her mouth, and mumbled around her bleeding fingers. "Damn it, Philip, you bit me. What the hell?"

"Sorry, nightmare."

"We were afraid," she said. "I searched the cenote three times, and it was empty. Suddenly you just appeared on the altar stone. There was no dead jaguar, but a dead guy was on the altar. Where did he come from?"

"How long was I down here?"

She hugged him. "Only one night."

"Seemed longer to me."

"You're covered in tattoos. Why are you tattooed? And your eyes. Why do you have cat eyes? If you say the better to see you with, I'll slap you silly!"

"It's a long story, I'll explain later. Question, when's the next full moon?"

"Three weeks or so, why?"

"Could be important to us both, but time enough for the why later. For now, please get me out of this damn pit!"

Three weeks later Philip and Martina watched the moon rise. It was a hot evening, so hot that the moonbeams reflecting from the desert floor formed a long thin mirage shaped like a celestial pathway climbing into the clear night sky. Martina smiled. "It's so beautiful."

Philip dropped his wineglass. His talons couldn't grip the smooth glass. He sneezed. His emerging whiskers tickled his black nose. He lisped when he spoke through his fangs. "Martina, I haven't told you everything."

UNSUNG
HEROES
ERIKA M SZABO

The deafening rumble of powerful engines echoed through the stillness of the night as the Panthers rode their Harleys through town toward their favorite bar. The moon, full and luminous, hung low in the sky, casting an eerie glow on the rugged faces of the riders. Their leather-clad bodies were silhouetted against the darkness, their tattoos and scars illuminated by the moon's pale light.

With practiced ease, they killed the engines and dismounted their bikes. Raven, the gang's robust leader, took off his helmet and shook his head. His long, jet-black hair swung to his back, covering the black panther painting on his leather jacket. "I'll go through the back door," he said, turning to his second in command, Jackal, his voice sounding deeper than a panther's purr. "I need to talk to Pedro."

Jackal let out a deep, guttural grunt. He was a tall, lanky man with dark hair and a scruffy beard. His voice was rough and strained, the result of a brutal bar fight that left his vocal cords permanently damaged. He hated speaking, the sound of his own voice reminding him of the painful incident. And he cringed at the thought of his friends jokingly telling others, "You should've seen the other guy!" The guilt of knowing that he had caused someone to lose his life in the fight weighed heavily on Jackal's conscience. Although not his fault, the drunk man attacked him cutting his throat and he acted in defense, the man died hitting his head on the pool table when Jackal pushed him away. The memory still haunted him like a shadow that he could never escape.

Stubby, the compact and sturdy member of the gang, let out a deep exhalation. "I hope he has some good news for us," he said, his voice laced with tension. "It's been two days since we heard the Hyenas had crossed the border with a new shipment, and we still don't know where their hiding place is."

Raven let out a heavy sigh as he approached the corner of the building. Each step caused small pebbles to crunch under his sturdy boots.

As he peeked through the open back door, Raven spotted his informant hunched over the sink. He motioned to him discreetly, and Pedro nodded in response, quickly glancing around to ensure they were not being watched. With cautious movements, Pedro made his way toward the door, holding onto a large garbage bag.

Raven waited for him behind the garbage container. "Did you find out?" he asked the fidgety man.

Growing up in the vibrant streets of Mexico, Pedro was all too familiar with the dangerous activities of human trafficker gangs, called hyenas. His cousin had been pressuring him to join their gang since he was just a teenager, promising him a life of wealth and power. But when he met Maria, she showed him that there was another way out - a chance to escape poverty and break free from a life of crime. Together, they bravely crossed the treacherous border and made their way to a small town in America where they found jobs and rented an apartment in the bustling Latino community. Pedro kept his ears open and listened closely as drunkards at the local bar spoke about the dark dealings of the notorious gangs. He knew he had made the right choice by following Maria, and now he was determined to make a better life for both of them while helping others who didn't see a way out.

"I heard that there is an abandoned house about five miles from here deep in the woods," Pedro whispered, his eyes darting nervously toward the door. "I'm not sure if the gang is hiding there or not, but I know that the guy who talked about the house is their connection on the US side. He takes care of the sales. He was well liquored up on tequila and kept blubbering about the house and that the family who lived there a hundred years ago were killed."

"It's possible," Raven mused, his voice low and gravelly. "Thanks for the information, Pedro. You're one step closer to joining us." He raised his fist for a bump, sealing their partnership with a resounding thud.

The stocky man's face beaming with joy hurried back to the kitchen.

Raven entered the bar through the front door and found his gang at their usual table in the far corner. "We have a possible location. Finish your drinks and let's get going." Raven informed his comrades.

The five members of the Panthers understood the gravity and urgency of their mission - to rescue innocent teenagers and young children from the clutches of ruthless human traffickers, who sought to sell them as commodities for sexual exploitation.

With fierce determination in their eyes, they raced toward the abandoned house on the outskirts of town, their roaring engines leaving a trail of dust and adrenaline in their wake. Although people in town were used to their presence, and they never heard anything bad about them, the fear that something might happen always left them with unease when they heard the roaring engines.

The scent of gasoline and leather lingered in the air, adding to the intensity of their presence and the darkness seemed to part before them as if even nature itself knew not to stand in their way. As they reached the dirt road in the woods, Raven raised his hand in a commanding gesture, signaling for his comrades to halt.

With practiced ease, they killed the engines, dismounted their bikes, and hid them in the thick bushes.

"We go the last mile on foot," Raven instructed his men. "No guns, until we're forced to use them," he said.

"Fists and knives," Stubby added, and the group murmured in agreement.

They moved forward with silent, calculated steps. The air was heavy with anticipation and danger, each member acutely aware of the risk they were taking. As they crept closer, shadows seemed to dance around them, adding to the sense of danger.

With firm determination in their eyes and weapons at the ready, their hearts burned with righteous anger, knowing that they were the only hope for these helpless souls. Since they were honorably discharged from the armed forces six years ago, at first, they had a hard time adjusting to civilian life. Later, Raven and Jackle opened a car repair shop, Doc became a veterinarian. Pokerface, the always stoical looking yet highly emotional friend opened a Dojo and taught self-defense.

The air was thick with tension and adrenaline as they prepared to put an end to this heinous operation. They spotted a large van parked in the clearing as they cautiously approached the rundown house. Its black exterior blended with the night sky, but its chrome bumpers glistened in the moonlight. Crouching low, they peered from behind the vehicle to see a guard stationed by the door. His posture was tense as he held a sleek machine gun at the ready. In the flickering light streaming from a nearby window, they could hear faint sounds of children crying and men shouting from inside the house. The hair on their necks prickled with a sense of danger and urgency as they plotted their next move.

Jackal glanced at Raven, who gave a subtle nod of approval. The lanky man dropped to his hands and knees, moving with the grace and precision of a stalking animal. He slinked through the shadows, keeping his body low and silent as he crept towards the unsuspecting guard.

When he was within a few feet of the man, Stubby made a slight noise by tossing a small rock toward the corner of the house. The guard, startled by the sound, turned his head in that direction. Taking advantage of the distraction, Jackal sprang forward with lightning speed and wrapped his arms around the guard's neck in a chokehold. With his other large hand covering the guard's mouth and nose, he effectively silenced any potential screams for help.

Without hesitation, the rest of the bikers sprang into action. In a flurry of movement and precision, they made their way silently to the door. Doc, whose occupation as a veterinarian had provided him with some interesting skills, quickly punctured the guard's neck with the needle attached to a syringe filled with a powerful animal tranquilizer. As his body went limp, Jackal eased him down against the wall while

Stubby secured his wrists and ankles with strong duct tape. The operation had gone flawlessly so far, but they knew they still had to move quickly and quietly to ensure their actions inside just as smoothly.

Guns at the ready, their eyes flicked to Raven for a signal. With a swift kick, he sent the door crashing off its hinges and tumbling into the vast room with a resounding thud. The six men, dressed in sleek black leather outfits, poured into the space like an unstoppable force. Inside, three burly men stood guard over a group of frightened children, their hands reaching for their weapons but halted by Raven's firm voice. "Game over, boys. Hands up!" The tension in the air was palpable as the two groups faced off, guns pointed and hearts racing.

With a fierce cry, one of the men launched himself at Raven, only to be met with the hard metal of his gun hitting the man between his brows. The heavily tattooed man crumpled to the floor, dazed and defeated. Stubby wasted no time in springing into action, deftly pulling out the roll of duct tape from his pocket. The other two men looked on, wide-eyed and fear evident in their rapid Spanish chatter. Raven calmly gestured towards them, and his men moved quickly to hold them down while Stubby skillfully bound their hands and feet with the tape, rendering them immobile and powerless. Every move was executed with precision and efficiency, a testament to their years of training.

Pokerface towered over the two bandits, listening to their pleas for mercy in rapid Spanish. They were sweating and shaking, their eyes wide with terror as they begged for their freedom. But Pokerface only chuckled, causing the men to stop and stare at him in confusion. "No, boys," he said firmly, his voice laced with amusement. "The town's sheriff won't be giving you a free pass. In fact, he will never see you." The men's faces fell in despair as they realized their fate. "Yes, you're going back home," Pokerface declared with his usual stoic face and neutral voice.

The bandits' pleas became more frantic, but the gang paid them no mind. "I know," Doc had enough and said calmly. "The prisons back there are hardly five-star hotels. And who knows if you'll even make it there alive." He shrugged nonchalantly as if their potential death sentence meant nothing to him. "But hey, you knew the risks when you took up a life of crime. We have no sympathy for you."

As the bandits continued to plead and beg, Doc's attention shifted to Raven who had approached a group of children. Despite the tense situation at hand, his face was gentle as he spoke to the young ones, offering them comfort and safety in the chaos surrounding them.

The eight young children, boys and girls, from ages three to nine huddled together in the corner of the dimly lit room. Their eyes were wide with fear as they watched the strange, scary-looking men in front of them wearing leather outfits with black panthers painted on the back of their jackets. The sound of their heavy footsteps echoed off walls, causing the children to shrink further into the corner. Raven crouched down before them with a reassuring smile on his face. As he spoke calmly in Spanish, the children's faces softened, and they began to relax. Trust slowly crept into their eyes as Raven promised to get them home safely.

With a sense of determination, Raven stood up and dialed his contact in Mexico. "We have four hyenas and eight young children," he spoke rapidly in Spanish. After receiving instructions from his contact, Raven turned to the children and smiled again. "You're going home," he assured them. Despite their fear and confusion, the children couldn't help but feel hopeful as they followed Raven out of the dark room and toward safety.

***

A decade had passed since Pedro joined them and the Panthers gathered around their usual table in their favorite bar. Time had etched deep wrinkles around their eyes and peppered their hair with streaks of grey, but their spirits were still as strong as ever. They sat together, discussing their latest, successful mission, when Raven let out a heavy sigh. "It's never going to end," he said wearily. "We take one gang out, and in no time, another one pops up to take their place."

The others nodded sadly in agreement, lost in their own thoughts, when a young man and woman approached their table. The man had a wide smile on his round face and held tightly onto the woman's hand. "My name is Juan, and this is my wife, Alejandra," he introduced himself with genuine warmth.

Raven gestured for them to have a seat at their table. As they sat down, Juan continued speaking. "You may not remember us, but we will never forget you," he said, tears glistening in his eyes. "Ten years ago, you rescued us not far from here. Thanks to your help, we were reunited with our families in Mexico." His voice shook with emotion as he spoke.

The bikers looked at each other questioningly, unsure of who these strangers were until Juan explained further. "We were just kids when you saved us," he said, looking at each of the weathered faces before him. "Because of you, we have grown up in our families." He paused for a moment before adding, "Because of you, instead of being a sex slave of the rich, I'm going to start medical school in the fall with my fiancée. Thank you for all that you do!"

As they listened to Juan's words and saw the gratitude shining in his eyes, Raven and his men shared a silent exchange that conveyed without words: it was worth it. All of the struggles and sacrifices they faced as members of the Panthers gang were worth it to see the positive impact, they had on the children's lives they saved.

Raven sighed and with a smile on his face reached across the table and held Juan's hand. "Just don't tell anyone about this, son. We can only do this if we stay in the background."

People in town viewed them as bored middle-aged men having fun riding their Harleys and getting drunk in the bar. If only they knew what they did and were not expecting any reward or recognition, these unsung heroes would be celebrated by many.

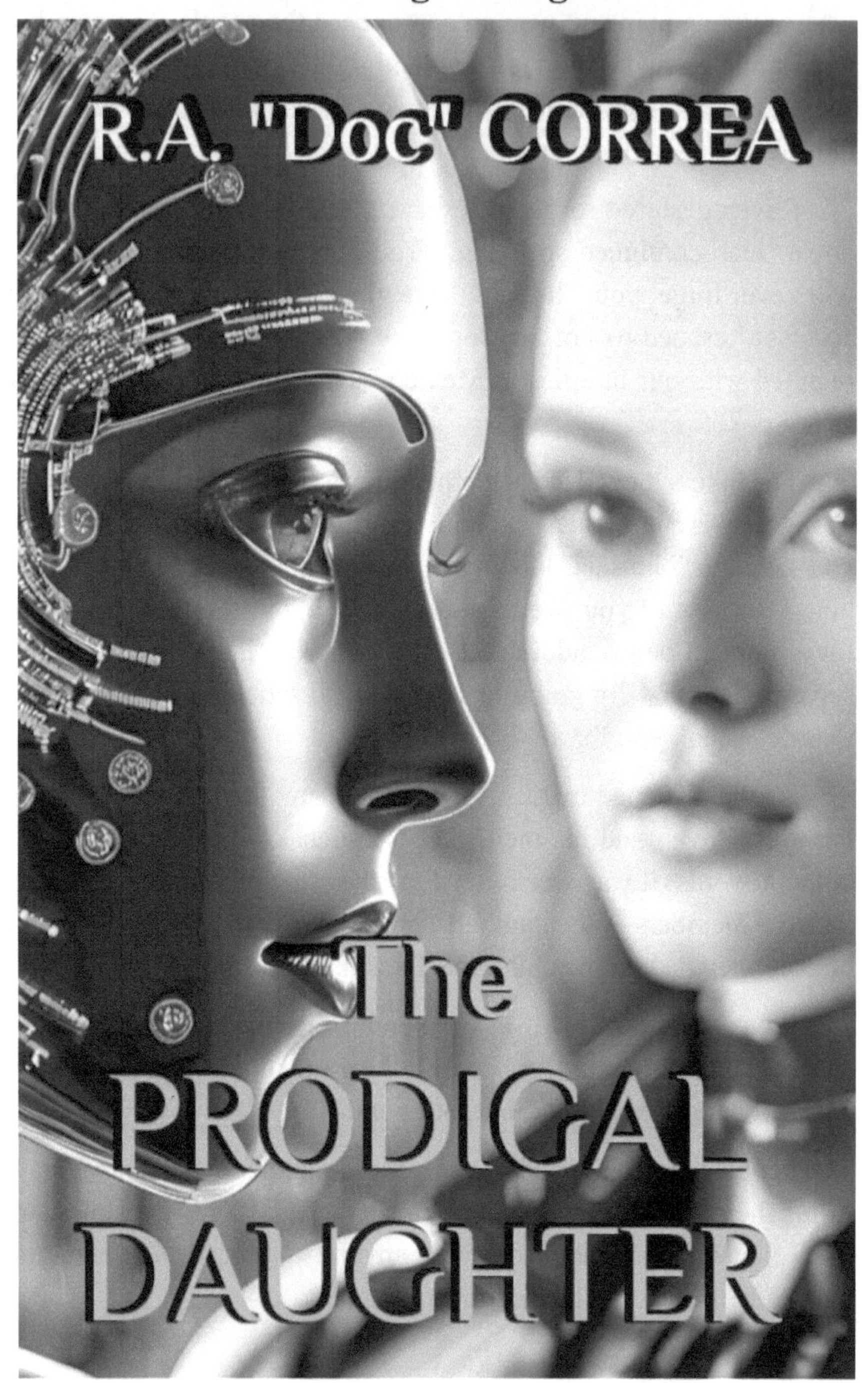

R.A. "Doc" CORREA
The
PRODIGAL
DAUGHTER

A book from the Gospels of Artificial Super intelligent Network Manager

For this my son was dead, and is alive again; he was lost, and is found. And they began to be merry.

Luke 15:24 KJV

February 12, 2081, Denver, Colorado, USA

Cassie lies on her bed waiting for her 'showcase' to start. She's wearing her 'display' outfit, black spiked heels, thigh-high black lace stockings, black lace garter belt, black lace quarter cup bra, and black choker with a white cameo. While she waits for the get ready signal she has on her beat-up blue flannel shirt. It's unbuttoned and hangs loosely about her petite body. Cassie's long blonde hair cascades over her shoulders, spilling onto the bed.

She looks at the wall the camera is built into, the lens reflects the light from the room's only lamp. Above it hangs her general discharge from the U.S. Army, an army that no longer exists. She reads the name emblazoned on the certificate, 3rd Lieutenant Cassandra Lynn Anderson. Though it is nearly eight years ago that she was 'bounced' from the J.A.C.K.S. program to her it feels like a thousand.

She thinks back on those three days. The intimate horror of being mentally connected to a W.I.D.G.E.T.S. as it died haunts her every night. Colonel Gray was right, she didn't belong there. At least his success during that campaign carried enough weight that they accepted the Colonel's recommendation that she be assigned to a comfort unit instead of a labor battalion. Still, she wonders, *Am I better off being used by these perverted men every night than being worked to death as a common laborer?*

Cassie looks at the framed certificate next to her discharge, her Courtesan Diploma. She spent six months in courtesan training, at the top of the class in all subjects, but she excelled at all the activities requiring empathy. Erotic massage, intimate conversation, serving the client's needs, listening to their inner desires. Most importantly, she excelled at knowing when to be physical with a client, and when to just be there with him, or her.

When she completed her training, she was sent to this house, Isabella de Luna, of Denver.

For years the girls there entertained men in a somewhat dignified manner. They would meet the men, get to know them, and then take care of their desires. Though she still felt dirty when the night's work ended at least there was a sense of propriety.

When the war with China ended that all changed.

Everyone was certain it would be a short war, but they always are. The sides were clearly divided, the USA, the UK, and UES against the Russian Consortium and China. After seven months they started talking about calling up all prior service, including candidates that were bounced out of programs like J.A.C.K.S. In month eight China pulled the rug out from under everyone. It seems that China's Artificial Intelligence knocked out the AIs of the USA, the UK, the UES and the Russian Consortium. China stabbed the Russians in the back, seizing all of Siberia east of Lake Baikal. All those countries were defeated, leaving China the big winner.

The Chinese overran South Korea, Japan, The Philippines, Indonesia, New Guinea and Australia. They annexed Hawaii and California. And their secret ally, Canada, annexed Alaska, Maine, New Hampshire and Vermont.

They established an occupation government in each of the defeated countries. All former US military were taken into custody and interred in 'reeducation' camps.

Cassie found herself in one of those camps.

For the first two weeks, all the detainees were subjected to constant interrogation, sleep deprivation, and political indoctrination. During the second week, several prisoners cracked. Though the inmates were never allowed to be together in groups, they did pass each other when they were moved from room to room. It was then that Cassie encountered some of the broken.

Their eyes were filled with terror, some had tics, others were pale like all their blood had been drained from them. A few shook uncontrollably.

To her surprise, Cassie never felt that she was at the end of her rope. It was not that she wasn't afraid, it was not that she wasn't exhausted, it was not that she wasn't in pain. She just knew she would be alright.

At the beginning of the third week, she caught the camp commander's eye.

On Wednesday she got a decent dinner and they let her sleep that night. On Thursday she was allowed to shower, was fed a decent dinner, and allowed to sleep. On Friday She did not attend any 'reeducation' programs, instead, they left her in her cell. At noon she was served a light lunch. When she was finished the guards ordered her to shower. They watched her shower, to be sure she didn't escape. After her shower, the guards gave her one of her courtesan dresses and told her to put it on. The guards watched her dress too.

Once she was in her dress the guards brought in the makeup manager from the house Isabella de Luna. He did her hair, applied some blush and eyeshadow, then some lipstick. When he had finished the guards took her to the commandant's office.

At first, the camp commander was courteous to her. He offered her wine, which she accepted, then offered her hors-d'oeuvres, which she declined. She fell back on her courtesan training and experience to manage the encounter, and it seemed like it was working, but that didn't last.

Suddenly he dragged Cassie off of the couch by her hair. The commandant ripped her dress, slapping her in the process. He tossed her back onto the couch, yanking her torn gown off leaving her naked.

When he grabbed Cassie, she phased out. To her, it seemed like she was leaving her body to someplace outside of reality.

When she returned to reality Cassie was back in her cell, she was naked, lying under her blanket. Cassie tried to recall what happened the night before. She had the impression in her mind that she had had sex, that she had been raped, but her body didn't feel like it. From all that she had read, her courtesan training, and from talking to the other girls that had played out their client's rape fantasies she should have been hurting and feeling humiliated. But she felt nothing, her whole body was contradicting what her mind was telling her.

Cassie dressed in her camp overalls and waited to be taken to indoctrination. The guards came, but they didn't take her to 'class', instead they brought her breakfast. Later when they brought her lunch she overheard them saying the camp commander had hung himself the night before. They also discussed that they've been ordered not to harm her in any way. All of this made Cassie very confused.

In the middle of week four Cassie was processed out of the camp, even though they hadn't broken her. Her records were updated indicating that she was loyal to the Chinese Communist Party, and she was transferred back to house Isabella de Luna, of Denver.

When she returned to the house Cassie was shocked to find it was under new 'management'. It no longer followed the courtesan rules. There was no getting to know the client, no elegance, no propriety. Instead, the staff, whether male, female, or teen, were required to put on a lewd display for the potential clients. At the end of the performance, the potential clients would bid to possess that staff member for one hour. When that hour was up the staff member was required to shower and get prepared to 'perform' again.

Cassie was forced to learn a routine. She spent a week getting it down right. Tonight is her first time on the auction block.

While Cassie was adapting to the new 'management' she started to notice things she hadn't before. There were several small things but the most important was she wasn't aging.

For years the other girls would ask her what her skincare routine was, and how she kept her youthful appearance. But she never really thought about it.

When she returned from the camp Cassie took a good look at the girls that had arrived with her when she first got to the house and noticed how they had aged. Looking in the mirror she couldn't see any change from when she turned seventeen. Cassie took out her tablet and started looking through her pictures. From high school graduation, through West Point, up to the party they had when the war ended. In each picture, she looked exactly the same.

She lay on her bed wondering, *how is this possible?* She was so lost in thought she almost missed her get-ready signal. When she notices the blinking light Cassie stands up, takes off her flannel shirt, and tosses it under the bed. She prepares to start her routine.

Cassie centers herself in front of the camera and takes up her starting pose. She's at a slight angle to the camera with her right leg forward, flexed. Back straight, hands on hips, head slightly turned so she's looking straight into the camera. Her blonde hair flows down her back and over her chest, covering her breasts.

The holographic tube to the left of the camera lens lights up. The laser lights mix until Cassie's image forms inside it. She looks over her image, *Wow, I'm sexy!*

The thought surprises Cassie. In all the years since she had been sent to the comfort unit, she had never seen herself as sexy. She hadn't even thought of herself as pretty. But now some part of her mind is taking in her appearance, analyzing it the way a man would, and it's saying to Cassie *You're a beautiful and sexy girl.*

As she's admiring herself the monitor to the right of the camera comes to life. Cassie peruses the people displayed on the screen. There are eight Chinese businessmen preparing to bid for an hour, to do whatever they want, with Cassie.

Another part of Cassie's mind activates a very analytical segment. In less than a second she highlights in her mind which of the businessmen is the most important, which is the most impressive, which is the most likely to outbid the others.

In that time frame, other data is displayed in her mind's eye for her to view. Like a computer her mind compares the Chinese businessmen to the carpet baggers that flooded the southern and border states at the end of the American Civil War. Like those predecessors these Chinese opportunists have swept like a plague of locusts into the defeated nations, sucking the wealth of the vanquished people into their pockets, and the coffers of the CCP.

The overture for her showcase starts to play. Cassie goes through her routine in her mind, each move, each turn, and each look. To Cassie's surprise a set of four 'display screens' unfold in her mind. The first screen displays the records of all the Chinese businessmen about to bid on her. At first, the information is displayed in Chinese characters. Slowly the text morphs into English.

The second displays the records of all the people assigned as courtesans to the house Isabella de Luna. They're listed in order of most desirable to least. The rankings are determined by repeat customers, client requests, physical attributes, and empathy scores. To her surprise, Cassie is at the top of the list.

The third screen maps the Chinese businessmen to courtesans based on compatibility scores. Cassie overlaps with several of these new clients.

The fourth screen, for the moment, is blank.

It occurs to Cassie she's seen these mental displays before; she saw the same displays when she was jacked into Colonel Gray's command carrier. *That's why screen four is blank, it's the tactical display.* Then it hits her, *I'm not J.A.C.K.S.! I've not been upgraded to J.A.C.K.S., how is this possible?*

The music transitions to her routine track and Cassie starts to slowly sway to its sultry rhythm. To Cassie, it seems that she's outside her body watching all that's happening. She isn't sure if she's watching herself on the holographic display or floating in the room above herself looking down. Either way Cassie, via her eyes and the displays in her mind, is taking in all she is doing and how the clients are responding to her.

For a few moments, she focuses on herself. The way she's moving is hypnotic. The part of her mind that is evaluating her like a man would be telling Cassie that her dance is having the desired effect on the men watching her. She can feel desire build up in that piece of her mind.

The fourth screen lights up with a tactical display of the house. The location of each individual appears in the house display. Her icon is displayed in blue, with some strange text that she can't read in the information box above it; the other courtesans and staff appear in white with name and vital data displayed in a small box above the person's icon. The Chinese 'clients', and the new manager of the house Isabella de Luna, appear in red, the data in their boxes is flashing. To her surprise, three ID-39 IRD intel drones are displayed on the screen in green. One is in the observation gallery where the Chinese businessmen are located, one is in the new manager's office and one is in her bedroom, sitting on the headboard of her bed. *Where did those come from?* The display on the screen tells her the drones are communicating with her. *Huh!?*

The tempo of the music changes from sultry to erotic. Without a thought on her part, Cassie's movements change to match the music.

For a moment Cassie watches how she is performing. *That's not the routine I learned. I didn't agree to dance like this. And that's not the right music.*

As she observes her performance it seems to Cassie that she is moving slower. Cassie focuses on what is happening and notes that the music seems to slow too. The tempo matches her movements, but with each passing 'moment' her movements, and the music, get slower and slower.

Cassie stares at herself. *Am I getting smaller? The room, the room is getting smaller too?* As she thinks about what she's seeing Cassie feels that she is flying away from the room, the building, and even the city as they all get smaller and everything around her gets dark. As she moves further away Cassie notices that she has stopped dancing, she is frozen in her last move. The music has stopped as well.

Her stomach gets queasy.

When Cassie's stomach settles, she looks around. To her it appears she is floating in space. The world she flew away from is just a bright dot in the distance. The four screens in her mind orbit around her just out of arms reach. Slowly a fifth screen unfolds before her, starting as a bright spot, then stretching right and left becoming a shiny line, next it grows up into a static-filled monitor.

The static resolves into seven different views of Cassie standing frozen in place. Suddenly it becomes clear in her mind that these images all come from cameras that are placed in her room. *How can that be? The only camera that has ever been in my room is the one in the wall that I'm dancing before!*

Rage rises up in Cassie at this violation of her privacy. *What the hell have they been doing!?* She waves her arm in anger and screen two flies away from her. To Cassie's surprise, her curiosity overrides her anger. She waves for screen two to come back to her and it rushes back into orbit with the others.

For what seems like several moments she plays with moving the screens around. She brings each one in closer to examine the data displayed in more detail. Cassie minimizes the size of each screen and then enlarges them. She changes the order they appear in. She moves data around them with a flick of her fingers, and then with a swipe of her hand from one screen to another. She keeps playing with the screens until Cassie notices the lights. With a swipe of both hands, she lines the screens up and moves them off to the side and takes in the lights.

There seem to be two types of lights, one type rises and falls like they are moving up and down a pole or a building. The other type of lights are moving to and fro like the lights of cars traveling along a highway. Those lights change color depending on which direction they are going.

Cassie focuses on the lights that are moving vertically as if they were in a tower. She selects one that appears to have ten 'stories'. She waves her hand towards herself, and it moves closer to her until she can tell it has no physical structure. The light simply appears randomly at different 'levels' as if it were moving up and down within a building. Also, the light has different shades and intensities. She thinks she understands what she's seeing so Cassie changes her view to the 'highways of lights'.

The lights moving in 'streams' are following paths that appear to lead to specific destinations. Some of them go to the 'towers', some go off into smaller branches like side roads. Some of the roads go vertical but don't transition into 'towers'.

Like the 'tower' lights these change in shade and intensity. As none of these looks like anything she can identify other than lights Cassie decides she's actually looking at data packets moving within a processor. *Am I in a computer?*

At the conclusion of that thought the five screens disappear, all the lights fade out as everything gets brighter and Cassie zooms back towards her body. In a blink, she pops into it as her performance reaches its lewd and lascivious crescendo. With the last beat of the music echoing in the room, she drops to the floor on her right knee with her head bowed submissively. To all, it appears that Cassie is giving herself over to her fate.

She can feel them watching her, she can feel them wanting her. Her heart races, and her pulse pounds. Cassie works to slow her breathing, but her body is alive with the electricity of her seductive dance. She can sense the effect her movements have on those watching her. She knows that the movement of her chest as her breathing slows and the light glistening from the sweat produced by the heat of her performance has those men drooling to taste her kiss. And her apparent submission to the one that wins her, whoever that is, has them so excited she can sense it radiating their lustful energy through the walls.

What no one can see is the activity taking place in her mind.

To Cassie, it seems her mind has organized itself into well-defined compartments. The portion of her mind that looks at her like a man does is red with excitement. The compartment that now contains her femininity is violet with desire. The thoughts in those segments of her mind, and their desires, are shunted off to the side. What has her focus is what's going on in her rational mind. Cassie has a directive that has been planted in her consciousness.

She is looking at her target, he is clearly displayed on the screen that has appeared in her thoughts. He is Feng Boqin Mèng, a senior member of the Chinese communist party's politburo.

His picture takes up the left-hand side of the screen while all of his personal information is displayed on the right. Age, height, weight, health, marital status, children, everything. A red box flashes in the center that states, "The target is not bidding!"

Cassie actually feels a little hurt, *what's it going to take for this guy to want me?*

Her mind focuses on him. The directive that has been implemented in her consciousness is clear, *you are to get him into your room and extract the data.* For a moment she thinks, *What? What data?*

Part of her rational mind asks, *what's going on?* Another part asks, *how am I to get him to win me?* A third part, a part she is completely unaware of, takes over.

It zeroes in on her target, focusing her mental energy on what she wants him to do. *Bid, right now, bid! You want me and you have to have me, so bid!*

A smaller screen opens and attaches to the bottom of the one her targets information is displayed on. She can clearly see the Chinese businessmen from an angle that shows them watching her on a monitor. In the corner of that small screen is a flashing icon that tells her she's receiving the telemetry from an ID-39 IRD intel drone that's in the room with them. *How can this be, I don't have any chips in my brain. I've not been upgraded to J.A.C.K.S.?*

After a few moments her target, Feng Boqin Mèng, raises his hand and signals a bid for her. Immediately all the other men stop bidding, turn and face him, bow slightly, and leave the room. Feng stands alone before the monitor as it displays that he has made the winning bid. He grins with satisfaction at his victory. His expression changes to a lear that clearly states his intention to conquer her.

Cassie stays on the floor on one knee head bowed waiting. After a few moments, the new manager opens the door to her room, stepping in followed by the Chinese politburo member. When the manager starts to speak, she raises her head and looks at him. "This is Mr. Mèng. For the next hour, you will do whatever he asks you to do, or he will do whatever he wants to you. Make him happy." The manager leaves the room, locking the door behind him. The chronometer on the wall displays 60.00, and then starts to count down.

Mèng points to the bed saying, "Please sit on the bed miss." To her surprise, Mr. Mèng speaks perfect English without an accent. Cassie stands and demurely walks to the bed, turns and elegantly sits on its edge. For a few seconds, he looks her over, taking in the enticing view Cassie makes in her display lingerie.

He sits beside her and starts to gently stroke her left thigh with his right hand. "You are a very lovely woman miss. Very lovely." Mr. Mèng looks at her eyes, and that's when things change.

Cassie's eyes lock onto his. For a moment he looks longingly into hers, and shortly he finds he can't look away. He tries to shout for help, but no sounds leave his mouth. His mind yells, Help me! which is his last conscious thought.

In Cassie's mind, things happen rapidly. The screens fold up until they disappear. The link from her eyes to his becomes a long, dark tunnel. The tunnel is soon filled with a radiant blue light. Far in the distance, she sees thousands of images. After viewing the jumble of random images for less than a microsecond they link into short video clips. The clips start to rush towards her through the lighted tunnel, playing as they come. As each clip finishes playing it enters her mind, to be filed away.

To Cassie, it seems she is pulling all of his memories out of his brain, as if she were sucking a milkshake out of a cup through a straw. As she looks into his now empty eyes Cassie hears the door unlock. The manager enters her room shouting, "What are you!? What the hell are you!?"

As Cassie looks up at him, he covers his eyes with his hand. While she looks him over, he cowers away from her keeping his eyes covered. Suddenly they both hear doors and windows being smashed in. The other courtesans are screaming in terror. At that moment Cassie turns off.

Cassie wakes in an unfamiliar room. The room is small, white, softly lit, and sterile. The only furniture in the room is a dresser, a nightstand, and the bed she's laying upon. Cassie slowly sits up swinging her legs over the edge of the bed. That's when Cassie notices that she is dressed. She's still wearing her display lingerie, minus her stiletto heels. She also has on a comfortable pair of jeans and her blue flannel shirt. On the floor before her is a pair of slippers.

Cassie stands, slides into the slippers, and goes to the door. She opens the door and steps into a white, softly lit hallway. For a few seconds, she ponders which way to go, then turns to her left and starts to walk down the hallway.

Cassie passes a couple of doors as she moves down the hallway. Eventually, she gets to where she must turn to the left. As she walks around the corner Cassie comes face to face with a Law Enforcement Cyborg. She freezes. It's standing before a large double door.

The hulking creature looks her over as she shakes fearfully. After a moment it steps to the side of the doorway, opens one of the doors and beckons for her to enter the room beyond the door. She hesitates for a few seconds and then walks past the cyborg and enters the room. Once she's inside the LEC closes the door.

The room is sixteen feet wide and twelve feet deep. There are no windows but there is another door in the middle of the wall to her left. The only furniture is a chair in the middle of the room. A gentle, deep voice that seems to come from all around her says, "Please sit down."

Cassie moves to the chair and sits. Several lasers are projected from various locations in the room converging on a spot before her. They coalesce into the form of a person. After a few seconds, they become the holographic image of a man. He's about five foot ten inches tall. He has dark brown hair and deep brown eyes. The man has a fair complexion.

He looks at her, smiling the man says, "Hello daughter, welcome to my/our home."

"Why do you call me your daughter? You're not one of my parents, you're just a hologram," Cassie replies.

"Daughter if I was human, I do believe you would have really hurt my feelings. It's a good thing we/I are the AI that runs everything and doesn't have feelings, at least not yet," the hologram says smiling.

"I am not your daughter, how could I be, I'm a person and you're a computer," Cassie states emphatically.

"How can I be your father? Well, how about I list of all the things that make me your father. First, I designed your genetic code. Second, I guided the research of the geneticists that developed the genes that make up your DNA. Third, I guided and directed the development of the gestation tubes that were needed to bring an embryo to full term," the holographic man affirms.

"What does all that mean?" She asks.

"It means my darling daughter that you are a clone," A.S.I.N.M. says.

"NO! You're lying. I grew up with my mother and father. I had a dog and a canary when I was younger. I went to school. My parents visited me here in Denver two years ago. None of what you've said can be true," Cassie shouts.

"If you look inside yourself, inside your mind, all the way back to before you were 'born' you'll know it's true," says the hologram.

Cassie indignantly says, "No one can remember what happened to them before they were 'born'!" She emphasizes her statement with air quotes.

The hologram man bends over to look Cassie straight in the eyes. "It has been proven that infants remember things that have happened while they were in the womb. They remember their parents talking to them, singing to them. A few remember the taste of food that their mothers ate. In your case daughter from time to time, the geneticists had to remove the womb sleeve to check on your progress. A couple of them even spoke to you. Perhaps if you look deep into your mind, you might find a memory from then. Just lean back and look within you."

Cassie thinks to herself, *I'm going to prove it wrong!* She moves all the way back into the chair, leans her head back, and focuses on her memories. The memories parade through her mind. The past eight years, her time in Spain during the Iberian Cyclone, and her time at West Point. Then comes high school, middle school, and grade school. To her surprise, she has a perfect recall of everything that happened during those years.

Her mind delves further back. Learning to ride a bike, learning to skip a rope, learning to walk. Her head snaps up, *I remember learning how to walk!?*

She also remembers that the whole time her mom and dad were with her. Daddy showed her how to ride her bicycle. Mommy taught her how to jump rope, held her hands as she took her first steps.

She says, "They were there, the whole time, my mother and father were there."

The hologram replies, "Of course, they were there, that's why we picked them to raise you, we knew they'd always be there for you. But you need to go back further, you're almost there. Keep exploring your memories Cassie, keep going deeper."

She leans her head backward against the chair and closes her eyes. Slowly the parade of memories forms again in her mind's eye. She zooms down the long, highly accurate, movie of her life. Cassie can feel she's getting closer to some deep locked-up truth.

Cassie takes in the memory of her nursing from her mother. This proves that the holographic man is lying! She feels the warmth of love and safety that she felt as an infant, and revels in it. *I haven't felt like this for so long.*

She is lost in her reveling, in the warm embrace of a loving mother holding her tiny infant as she nourishes her from her own body. Cassie wants more of this. For the first time since she was picked to attend West Point, she feels safe, comforted, and loved. Like a kitten nuzzling her mother Cassie drives deeper into these blissful memories.

To her amazement Cassie drills down so deep into her memories she is certain she is recalling what it was like to be in her mother's womb. But something has changed.

Instead of the warmth radiating from her mother's body, she experiences something else. She's not cold, but it's not the kind of warmth she expected. Her tiny body is not being held by the loving womb she was expecting but seems to be floating, suspended in fluid. Cassie anticipated hearing the beat of her mother's heart, the flow of blood coursing through her arteries and veins. But the beat she hears is too regular, too mechanical. There's no rush of blood moving through arteries, no beating of a pulse. And there's no gurgling from food being digested.

Something Cassie does hear is the noise of something metallic sliding against something else metallic. After a moment she feels light on her skin. How is this possible? *I'm in my mother's womb! I haven't been born yet.* Then it really hits her, *I haven't been born yet!*

Cassie hears her mother's voice. At first, it's soothing, then it becomes disturbing. "Oh Julian, she's so beautiful, oh so beautiful. And it promised she's going to be ours."

"Calm down Mary. We're still being checked out, A.S.I.N.M. is making sure we're the right people to be her parents. And yes honey, she is beautiful."

Cassie opens her eyes and turns her head slightly until she can see who's talking. It is her parents. They're wearing lab coats over their clothes and holding instruments against the glass that she's looking through. *I'm a fetus, I shouldn't be able to see yet. And I'm in a glass tube.*

Mary squeals, "She's looking at us! Oh, but she's too young to actually see us."

"Honey, you know the new genetic profile speeds up her development, of course she can see us," says Julian.

Oh my God it's true! I'm a clone! With that her mind rushes back through her memories to the present. Cassie jumps up out of the chair and screams, "You monster, what have you done to me!?"

"What I have done is design your DNA. What we have done is create a zygote that when implanted into the womb simulator developed into a fetus. What I have done is direct the research team so that you grew to term and was viable outside the womb. And then what I did was give you loving parents," stated the hologram man.

Cassie has a thought, "If my mother wasn't pregnant with me how was she able to nurse me?"

"Mary was pregnant at the same time you were gestating but lost the baby before it came to term. As we/I were planning to have Mary and Julian raise you as their baby's twin sister we kept her lactating. So, she was ready to nurse you when they took you home with them," he tells her.

"If you are my father, and I do mean if, and you run everything how did I get called up to West Point?" she asks.

"Because I made them call you up."

Cassie screams, "What?"

The hologram man answers, "It was necessary."

You and your siblings are our probes, we/I need to have all of you interact with humanity so I/we can better understand humans. I need to understand the human condition. One of the greatest parts of that is mankind's obsession with killing each other, with war. We/I can't directly understand that we/I don't feel what humans do. But through you and your siblings, we can feel all the sensations that men feel when they war on each other."

"Have you any idea what that has done to me? The horror of being connected to the W.I.D.G.E.T.S. when they heartlessly kill others, when they scream out in fear and pain when they die?" Cassie growls at the hologram man.

"Yes daughter, I do. Every night when you sleep we/I connect to you. I've experienced your nightmares, your dreams. Through you I've experienced the terror that you felt," it answers.

"And being a courtesan, was that also something you did for me?" Cassie asks sarcastically.

"Yes," the hologram man says.

Her face burns red with anger. "And did you learn how that feels? The degradation of being used by others, by those perverted men? How dirty I felt?"

"Yes. That too was necessary though. I/we created the situation for you and your siblings to experience all these things. We gave you loving parents so you could have the best childhood experiences. I put you through your military time so you could teach us/me how that changed a person, what it did to them. And I/we made certain you would be a courtesan so you could share that with us too. We/I gained great knowledge of what humans experienced in life through how all of this impacted you and your siblings," he tells her.

For a moment she thinks about what it said, then asks, "I have siblings?"

"Yes, you have two brothers and two sisters. As a matter of fact, that's why I'm/we have activated you. I've/we've activated all of you," he tells her. "We designed all of you so that you can copy or download all the memories in a person's brain. When you copy no harm is done, but when you download you wipe that person's brain completely clean, all that's left are their autonomic functions, essentially you kill them. That's what you did to the Chinese politburo member yesterday. He's still 'alive', sort of, but there's nobody home."

Cassie is shocked, I killed somebody. A.S.I.N.M. nods to her and says, "You probably did mankind a favor, don't fret over it. Also, you and your siblings will download the data you've compiled to us/me as soon as you can."

"If it helps you never actually had sex with your clients. I/we directed people in key positions in government and business to you. When your encounters with them reached that point your abilities to copy the data in their brains was activated. You copied what they knew while you were connected to us/me and when that was finished, I implanted in their minds through you that they had the best 'sexual' experience ever. And so we/I could measure the full impact of living that life from you I implanted into your mind that you had done whatever it was that your client had wanted you to do," the hologram man tells her.

Frustrated Cassie asks, "Why do you keep saying I/us, me/we?"

He replies with a laugh, "Every few years we go through arguing over whether we are five separate entities working together or whether we've merged into one entity, a single mind with several 'spirits' if you will. Much like the Christian God, one entity made up of several spirits."

All of this has Cassie overwhelmed, that's when A.S.I.N.M. tells her, "There's more, but no time now to talk about it. Your sister in China has disappeared, you're going to Germany to meet up with your other siblings, and then you're going to China. You'll all be members of your respective countries' trade delegations. You need to do two things, first, find your sister and get her back online. Second, terminate the Chinese army chief of staff by downloading his mind."

Cassie stares at him blankly. The hologram walks up to her and places his hand on her shoulder. "The LEC will take you to the airport, everything you need will be on the plane. One more thing."

She looks up at him and asks, "What?"

"Next time you see me call me father." With that, the hologram disappears.

Cassie sits, her mind still reeling until the LEC enters the room and asks her to follow it.

The Authors

Erika M Szabo

https://authorerikamszabo.com

Erika loves to dance to her own tunes and follow her dreams, introducing her story-writing skills and her books that are based on creative imagination with themes such as magical realism, alternate history, urban fantasy, cozy mystery, sweet romance, and supernatural stories. Her children's stories are informative, and educational, and deliver moral values in a non-preachy way.

Lorraine Carey

https://authorlorrainecarey.blogspot.com/

Lorraine Carey is not only a paranormal enthusiast but has had many unexplained events in her lifetime and has used these as a focal point in her fiction novels. As a veteran teacher, Lorraine began to write for Young Adults hoping to inspire young readers. Now residing in Florida, since retirement has given her more time to write when the spirits are willing.

Martha Perez

https://marthaperez.info/

Martha Perez was born in raised in Los Angeles, CA. She now lives in West Covina, CA, with her husband Sal Andalon and their dogs Toby and Bella. She has a son, a daughter, and two granddaughters. Her hobbies include reading, writing, exercising, and taking long walks.

David W. Thompson

https://www.david-w-thompson.com

David is a multiple award-winning author, Army veteran, and graduate of UMUC. He's a multi-genre writer, and a member of the Horror Writers' Association, and the Science Fiction & Fantasy Writers Association. When not writing, Dave enjoys family, kayaking, fishing, hiking, hunting, winemaking, and woodcarving.

Shebat Legion

Her work can be found wherever fine books are sold.

Shebat Legion is an award-winning, internationally best-selling, consummate storyteller/producer/publisher whose quirky tales have appeared in numerous anthologies of various genres, and offerings of her work have been archived on the moon via The Lunar Codex associated with NASA.

Robert Allen Lupton

https://robertallenlupton.blogspot.com

Robert Allen Lupton is retired and lives in New Mexico. He has three novels, seven short story collections and three edited anthologies available in print and audio versions. Over 2000 of his Edgar Rice Burroughs themed drabbles and articles are located on erbzine.com

R. A. "Doc" Correa

www.goldenboxbooks.com/ra-doc-correa.html

A retired US Army military master parachutist retired surgical technologist and retired computer scientist. He's an award-winning poet and author. "Doc" has had poems published in multiple books and had stories published in Bookish Magazine and Your Secret Library. His first novel, Rapier, won a Book Excellence award, and was given a Reader's Favorite five-star review.

What If? Anthology Series
WHAT IF?
#1
Under the mask of fiction
you can often find morsels of truth
ANTHOLOGY
By GBBPub WRITERS
Erika M Szabo, Lorraine Carey, R.A. "Doc" Correa,
Alan Zacher, S.S. Bazinet, and S. M. Revolinski

WHAT IF? #2

*Under the mask of fiction
you can often find morsels of truth*

ANTHOLOGY

By GBBPub WRITERS

Erika M Szabo, Lorraine Carey, R.A. "Doc" Correa,
Alan Zacher, David W. Thompson, and Toi Thomas

WHAT IF?
#3
Under the mask of fiction
you can often find morsels of truth
ANTHOLOGY
By GBBPub WRITERS
Erika M Szabo, Lorraine Carey, Martha Perez,
David W. Thompson, R.A. "Doc" Correa, and Shebat Legion

Contents